THE SURGEON'S BABY

Kathleen Ryder

Copyright © 2021 Kathleen Ryder.

All rights reserved.

ISBN

This book is a work of fiction. Names, characters, places and incidents are either the product of the author's imagination or are used fictitiously, and any resemblance to actual persons, living or dead, business establishments, events or locales is entirely coincidental.

Except for use in any review, the reproduction or utilisation of this work in whole or in part in any form by any electronic, mechanical, or other means, now known or hereafter invented, including xerography, photocopying and recording, or in any information storage and retrieval system, is forbidden without the permission of the author, Kathleen Ryder.

Cover design by Kylie Sek of Cover Culture.

PROLOGUE

The door to the clinic burst open, a frantic Emma rushing through to the reception desk, her heart leaping in her throat, her pulse racing with panic. A problem, how can there be a problem? She was told everything was fine, that the procedure had gone to plan, she was flying home tomorrow!

"Emma, Doctor Delaney is expecting you, go straight through," the receptionist waved her hand vaguely in the direction of a hallway and turned back to her magazine. Emma tried to slow her steps, tried to force down the bile she could taste in the back of her mouth.

"Emma dear, come in," Doctor Delaney places a hand on Emma's back and ushers her through the doorway. "Can I get you anything? Tea? Water?"

"Thank you, I'm-" Emma stops mid-sentence as her eyes land on a second person, paused, framed in the doorway.

"Ah," Doctor Delaney follows Emma's gaze, clapping his hands together. "Ivan, come in, take a seat. Emma, this is Doctor Ivan Delgado, Ivan, this is Emma Roberts," he introduces nervously.

Emma's breath caught in her throat as she tried not to stare at Ivan. "Hi" Emma squeaks, her throat like sandpaper, voice wobbling, betraying her nerves.

"I know you must be worried Emma," Doctor Delaney smiles kindly at her, "and I apologise for being cryptic over the telephone, but I felt it was better to have this discussion in private, with all parties concerned." Emma gave herself a mental shake, and leant forward, nodding. "As you know, you requested insemination using an anonymous donor." Doctor Delaney perused her file on the desk in front of him. "I'm very sorry Emma, I'm not sure how to tell you this, but there was a terrible error in our laboratory, our technicians have somehow mixed up the samples. Instead of the anonymous donor you selected, you were mistakenly inseminated with a sample from a private donor, which was meant for storage only."

"I see." Emma's mind raced. What did he mean, a private donor? It was not really that bad, was it? "While I appreciate you telling me this as soon as you became aware of the error, it really makes no difference to me where the sample came from," Emma shrugs, trying to keep calm. "Unless the private donor has a hereditary medical condition, it doesn't change anything."

"Actually," drawls Ivan, leaning back in his chair and crossing his arms over his broad chest, "it changes everything."

"I don't understand, do you work in the lab?" Emma frowned in confusion, turning away from Ivan to face Doctor Delaney. "What exactly are you saying? Is there something wrong with the sample?" Emma was not sure she could stand to find out, the cost of this first procedure had eaten up all of her savings, if it didn't work...Well, she was not sure when, or even if, she would be able to cobble together enough funds to have another attempt.

"No, the sample is medically viable," Doctor Delaney shuffles the paperwork in Emma's file with a pointed look in Ivan's direction, "but it is complicated."

"He means," Ivan interjects dryly, fixing Emma with a scathing look, "that you are having my baby."

"You can't be serious." Emma felt the colour drain from her face as she sat looking from Doctor Delaney to Doctor Delgado and back again, her mouth gaping open.

"I have never been more serious in my life," Ivan's eyes narrow as he watches Emma fidget in her chair. "If you are pregnant, you will be carrying my child, and I expect to be involved every step of the way. Amicably or court-appointed," Ivan shrugged, "I don't care. No child of mine will grow up without their father." The warning in Ivan's voice was clear, and it sent shivers down Emma's spine.

"Emma," Doctor Delaney reaches forward to pat her hand, "it is too early for us to know, but if you are pregnant, Ivan will not only be the father of your baby, but as the two of you have no contract in place, Ivan will have full legal rights to this baby."

CHAPTER ONE

Emma turned as white as a sheet and for a brief moment, Ivan wondered if she might be about to faint. The reality of the situation she had brought upon herself he supposed. Well, she would get no sympathy from him, as far as he was concerned, there was only one reason that an unmarried woman would want to undergo the trauma of invasive In Vitro Fertilisation treatment alone, and that was if she intended to trap a man into marriage using a surprise pregnancy. Ivan found himself feeling pity for the poor man involved and hoped that he discovered the truth before it was too late. Emma couldn't breathe. She was all too aware of Ivan watching her, sizing her up. She wanted to slap him! She wanted to scream at the unfairness of her situation, she wanted to cry at the possibility of her dream slipping away. Mostly, she just wanted to flee, to run far away where no one would ever find her. How dare he! How dare he waltz in here and make claims on her unborn baby. Ivan's eyes narrowed as her hands slipped protectively across her stomach. If there was a baby in there, there was no way Ivan was taking over, no way at all!

Emma stood suddenly, her chair wobbling in protest. "Gentlemen," she nodded, "I have an early flight tomorrow that I need to prepare for. Doctor

Delaney, I will be in touch in a few weeks." Emma moved towards the door, scowling as Ivan stood to block her way.

"You can't seriously be leaving; we have things we need to discuss."

"Actually, we don't," Emma managed a tight smile. "I employed the services of this clinic in good faith. Any error made on their behalf is not my responsibility." She watched more than a little smugly as Ivan's mouth opened and closed wordlessly.

"Your logic, such as it is, will never stand up in court. If you are pregnant," he glanced at her stomach, "I will be the father, biology doesn't lie, and I think you will find that it tends to get quite a lot of support in court."

"Goodbye Ivan," Emma refused to rise to his veiled threats, stepping around him and walking out of the office, head held high.

"Emma," Ivan's tone was clipped, "I'll be in touch". Emma was not sure if that was meant as a threat or a promise, but either way, it sent rivers of chills down her spine.

Having returned directly back to her hotel from Doctor Delaney's office, Emma found herself too wound up to pack, instead, she donned her swimsuit, a turquoise one-piece, and took the lift to the roof to make use of the hotel's swimming pool. As she swam effortlessly up and down the length of the swimming pool, she felt the tension of the day start to ebb away. Would it be so bad, she wondered, if she was pregnant to Ivan? She imagined that a child could do a lot worse than to have a father like Ivan, at least he was employed. If nothing else, he did seem to be rather passionate, she mused. Of course, some would call that stubborn and pig-headed, she reminded herself sternly. By the time she dragged herself from the pool and wrapped a plush towel around her waist, she was no closer to an answer on Ivan than when she first arrived home. Exhausted, Emma returned to her room, ignoring the open suitcase on the coffee table and instead opting for the plump king-sized bed, stripping off her swimsuit and sliding naked between the Egyptian sheets, sleep claiming her almost immediately. Emma had a fitful night's sleep, plagued by weird dreams featuring Ivan, smiling at her while holding a baby, relieved when her alarm finally went off, sleepwalking through the motions of finally packing, showering and dressing, before heading down to the lobby to check out, the taxi she pre-booked already waiting for her.

It was a sleepless Emma that boarded the flight bound for Alice Springs, thankful that it was a Saturday, and that the flight was a direct route from Brisbane to Alice Springs. She had splashed out, seeing as it was a special occasion, the possible conception of her first child, and had redeemed her frequent flyer points for an upgrade to business class. She thought that she would feel posh, sitting in her business class seat as everyone trudged through to economy, but she actually felt awkwardly on display, as if everyone knew she didn't belong in this section of the plane. She wondered if Ivan travelled business class, deciding he probably did, he didn't strike her as the sort of person who would travel economy. She accepted a pre-flight glass of orange juice from the steward, more for something to do with her nervous hands than out of any real thirst and leant back to listen to the safety messages. Emma hated flying, always had. Take off terrified her, left her hyperventilating, tears streaking down her face. It didn't matter if she flew solo or with other people, she always had the exact same reaction each time, which caused her endless humiliation. Emma settled into the flight once the plane had levelled out, determined to enjoy what she imagined would be her first, and last, ride in business class.

It didn't matter where Emma holidayed, whenever she flew home, over the vast, barren desert landscape, it always took her breath away. The vibrant reds, rich oranges, surreal pinks, and grey greens of the landscape below fascinated her. The way the desert ebbed and flowed around hidden, long-forgotten waterways, the sparsely populated trees dotted haphazardly on the ground, the unexpected tracks that occasionally crisscrossed the land; it all called to her. As isolated and as remote as Alice Springs was, to Emma, it called to her, there was a real sense of belonging, of home here. Despite being born and raised a Brisbane City girl, Emma was not sure if she would ever live anywhere else now. As the plane banked, Emma was treated to her first sight of Alice Springs, the town nestled safely among the MacDonnell Ranges. It looked as she knew it would, dusty, bathed in a soft haze of sunlight, the perfectly clear skies overhead glaringly bright. A soft sigh escaped Emma's lips as the plane dipped lower, the trees and roads below growing bigger in the window. The landing was smooth, a nice surprise, and Emma stretched, watching as the stairs were wheeled to the plane doors. Once her luggage was collected, Emma looked around the terminal, trying to locate her younger sister, Rosalind. A flash of colour drew her eye and she turned towards the exit doors as a cloud of perfume enveloped her.

"Rosalind," Emma started, "thank you for picking me up."

"Don't be silly! Mother said I should just let you get a taxi like everybody else, but I had to take Scott to the golf club, so I was already out anyway." At thirty, Rosalind had the luxury of not looking a day over twenty-five. Her bubbly personality only added to the illusion. It was hard for Emma to remember sometimes that Rosalind was in fact married, and a partner in a prestigious law firm, she acted so childishly and scatterbrained. As much as she irked Emma at times, the two sisters were still close, quite a feat considering how much their parents pitted them against each other as children. Dennis and Patrice Roberts believed that everything in life was a competition, and they were only interested in spending their resources on the best of the best. While Rosalind attended after school activities and had private education, Emma had attended a local government-run school, spending her afternoons escaping to fantasy worlds within the pages of her books, or helping their housekeeper to make dinner. Emma had always known her parents favoured Rosalind and had long since given up trying to best her at anything. As much as her parent's behaviour stung, Emma couldn't fault her sister, who, despite everything, didn't have a nasty bone in her body.

The drive to Emma's house was a quick one, Emma filling Rosalind in on most of her time in Brisbane, omitting the real reason for the visit, her medical procedure, as well as her run-in with Ivan.

"I won't come in Em, I promised Dad I would swing past and look through some contracts he had drawn up while Scott is playing golf. He wants to diversify the business," Rosalind added offhandedly, unaware that Emma had no idea of their father's plans. "We'll do lunch sometime this week though, if that suits you?"

"Sounds good," Emma nodded, retrieving her suitcase off the backseat. Once she had waved her sister off, she made her way inside. Her house certainly was not fancy, not by anybody's standards, but it was hers, and that was all that mattered. A quick check of the house telephone on the way past revealed a total of zero messages, Emma wondered why she even had a house telephone.

Going through to the bedroom, Emma kicked off her flats and popped open her suitcase, dumping all of the clothes into a pile on the floor. With her few toiletries, books, and other knick-knacks put away in a matter of minutes, Emma stripped off all of her clothes, gathered the washing off of the floor, and dumped everything into the laundry hamper. A quick, refreshing shower, and some clean clothes, and Emma was ready to relax, making the most of her remaining few hours on holiday

before needing to return to work by binging her
favourite reality television show.

CHAPTER TWO

Ivan sighed in frustration. When would his parents learn that he was not interested in finding a wife? He was thirty-five for goodness sake! The last thing he needed was his mother playing matchmaker for him, if he wanted a wife, he would find his own, it was not as if he didn't have options, he did, he just was not interested in marriage. He tried to listen to what the woman opposite him was saying, he really did, but all he could think about was last week's mix up with Emma. Good grief, had it really only been a week?! On paper, the woman opposite was his ideal partner; professional, unmarried, tall, blonde, and socially conscious. The reality, however, was quite different. While she was indeed unmarried, tall, and blonde, she was only socially conscious when her developer father, and employer, demanded it, which, according to her, was only when there were tax breaks to be had. Ivan was not interested in fake people, he got enough of them with his job, a source of contention between him and his father. Edward Delgado couldn't understand why Ivan was so reluctant to join his practice, to become a partner in his father's clinic. The truth was, while being a surgeon once thrilled Ivan, it now leaves him bored. Instead of the life-changing trauma surgery he used to perform in Sri Lanka, he now deals with a steady stream of patients referred to his father's clinic for vanity treatments. He had become jaded and disillusioned, sentiments his father had no time for.

He had been stalling for weeks now, and as patient as his father was, he knew he would have to give him an answer soon. His mother thought that throwing any available woman she could find at Ivan would entice him to stay, but in actual fact, it was doing the very opposite. He was chafing to leave, it was not that he hated Brisbane, far from it, but he wanted to go where he could make a real difference, where the surgery he did could transform someone's entire life, not just give them a prettier nose. Despite his personal reservations, his father was not getting any younger, and Ivan had actually been considering his offer, if nothing else, being his father's partner at the clinic would mean that he would be closer to his family, should anything ever happen again, unlike last time. That is, until he received the telephone call from Doctor Delaney last week. Ivan could never have guessed that on such an innocent-looking Friday, the simple act of answering his telephone would have the potential to literally change his life. He was still reeling, if he was honest with himself, the scenario replaying over and over in his head. He was barely twenty when he made the decision all those years ago, to freeze his sperm for some later date. The future seemed so very far off back then. A medical student, full of self-importance, invincible against the world, he had been struck down with leukemia, and at the worst of it, his doctor had urged him to have a sample of his sperm frozen for later use, as a precaution. By the time Ivan had recovered and graduated, the sample had been forgotten about.

When Doctor Delaney called him last week, it was the first time Ivan had even thought about his sample in over a decade. Now, after rejecting the thought of a wife and kids in favour of dedicating his life to transforming the lives of others, it was a surreal situation to find himself in, knowing that, quite possibly, there was a woman out there, a relative stranger, who was now carrying his child. Ivan had been furious, had demanded to know how such an error could have occurred. Doctor Delaney had been unable to provide any answers, just as horrified as Ivan at the mistake. Ivan had thought that going down to the clinic, meeting this unknown woman, would make the situation easier. For a fleeting moment, Ivan had been prepared to simply meet this woman and her husband, sympathise with their predicament, and sign whatever paperwork he needed to sign to ensure that the woman and her husband were the legal parents, not Ivan. That all changed the minute Ivan discovered that she was, in fact, unmarried. Ivan was not a prude, nor was he old fashioned. He knew that single women had babies every day, as was their right, but there was no way any child of Ivan's, planned or not, would grow up without a father. Ivan strongly suspected that this woman was a charlatan, having been the subject of one such female himself previously, she had even gone as far as faking a sonogram to try to convince Ivan of impending parenthood. Once she realised that he would not marry just for the sake of a child, she had cut her losses and come clean.

"Ivan," the shrill voice of his date cut through his reverie. "Are you even listening to me?" Ivan winced, he had been too deep in thought to hear the question his date had asked him, and if the irritation in her voice was anything to go by, she had already repeated herself.

"I'm sorry Meghan," Ivan conceded, "I am not in the right headspace for any type of relationship right now." He drew some bills out of his wallet and laid them on the table. "Dinner's on me, I'm sorry you wasted your time." Ivan stood and nodded at Meghan. She really was very stunning, no doubt his mother would be most disappointed in how the evening had turned out. Ivan had walked to the restaurant tonight, it pre-empted the inevitable coy request for a lift home, and besides, he enjoyed walking, it helped clear his head and gave him time to think. Brisbane was its usual grey tonight; a cool breeze blew off the Brisbane River and made Ivan wish he had thought to bring a jacket. Living right on the river, it was not long until Ivan was sliding his key into the front door of his penthouse apartment. Ivan loved his apartment, from the full-length windows on two sides to the sunken master bathroom, it was the one luxury Ivan was not willing to compromise on. He was used to working long hours for months on end in far-flung countries like Sri Lanka, on the rare times he came back to his Brisbane base, he liked to spoil himself, it was his reward for all the times he had to rough it.

Emptying his pockets onto the granite kitchen countertop, Ivan bypassed the house telephone and crossed through to his study, switching his laptop on and opening up his emails. He scrolled through the dozens of new messages that had come in while he was out, eyes scanning for a specific sender, dropping into his desk chair and clicking open once he had found it. He skimmed the message quickly, a slow smile spreading across his face as the news sunk in. He read the message through again, slowly so as not to miss anything, before flexing his fingers and hitting reply. Ivan felt as if the weight of the world had been lifted off his shoulders. Finally, a way out of Brisbane, in such a way so as not to hurt his father, who, Ivan knew, really did have his best interests at heart. He knew from Doctor Delaney that Emma worked at the Alice Springs hospital, although he was not sure in what capacity, and after that, it was a simple case of reaching out to a former colleague who now worked at the Alice Springs hospital as the Chief Medical Officer, Doctor Robert Curtain. The email Ivan just replied to was confirmation of a job offer as a trauma surgeon on a twelve-month placement, starting as soon as he could arrive. Ivan checked outgoing flights from Brisbane, intending to leave as soon as possible, but first, he had to call his father.

In the end, Ivan was not able to get away for another week, his father was a little disappointed but understood Ivan's restlessness. It was with renewed excitement that Ivan boarded his plane early Wednesday morning, bound for Alice Springs. A weekday flight meant rather a long detour via Coffs Harbour, Ivan would not land until mid-afternoon, but he had not wanted to wait even one more day to leave. Ivan's flight was uneventful, once at Coffs Harbour, however, a mechanical issue meant the stopover was delayed by several hours, meaning his arrival into Alice Springs happened after the airport had closed for the night. By the time Ivan had disembarked, found a taxi, and arrived at the hospital, it was after dark. The only thing he wanted was to locate the switchboard office, collect his accommodation pack, and crawl into bed. Everything else would have to wait until tomorrow.

CHAPTER THREE

By the time Wednesday rolled around, Emma was well and truly ready for another holiday! It was hard to believe that she had already been back at work for two weeks, it felt like an eternity. These sixteen-hour shifts were killing her! It was the bane of working at switchboard, they were perpetually short-staffed. Instead of the required six staff members, they currently only had three, meaning there was no room for a reprieve, all three staff members were working non-stop sixteen-hour shifts for the foreseeable future. Emma had drawn the short straw, the 8pm to 8am shift, minimal staff and patient interactions, but the most paperwork and filing. It was time-consuming and tedious and gave Emma far too much time to think. She had just ducked into the adjoining kitchenette to make herself a strong cup of coffee when there was a soft knock on the switchboard window.

"I'll be right there," she called out, switching the kettle on to boil. Smiling as she stepped out into the office, Emma froze, her smile slipping, mouth gaping open. "You!" she gasped, stunned at the sight of Ivan standing at her window. "What are you doing here?"

Seeing Emma standing at the switchboard window was enough to make Ivan believe in luck or fate or whatever other name people wanted to call it. Ivan raised an eyebrow questioningly. "Is that how you greet all of your new doctors?"

"New doctors? You?" Emma gasped. "No! You are Ivan Delgado?" she looked at him sceptically. Her mouth had gone very dry, the prayers for the telephone to ring went unanswered.

"I see my reputation has preceded me," Ivan wondered just what exactly it was that Emma had heard about him, and whether or not it was actually the truth. "I was told that switchboard would have my accommodation pack ready for collection..." Ivan trailed off, an unspoken question lingering between them.

Emma stared at Ivan, refusing to break eye contact, until finally, blinking, she spun on her heel and stalked over to a nearby cupboard, ripping the door open and rummaging around inside. She returned with a manilla envelope which she pushed through the small opening at the base of the switchboard window. "Here, your accommodation pack." Ivan's hand snaked out and captured her fingers before she had a chance to move them, the contact causing a gasp to escape her lips before she could stop it. Blue eyes clashed with brown, Emma thought that Ivan looked tired, and she felt a momentary pang of remorse for being curt with him. Before she could apologise, Ivan stepped back, releasing her fingers.

"Thank you, Emma, have a nice night."

Ivan didn't sleep a wink. Instead, he lay awake all night, replaying the moment he had held Emma's hand. Although only briefly, it had sent a shockwave of electricity and awareness coursing through Ivan's veins. How on Earth could he be attracted to someone like her? It made no sense; she was not his type. Hell, she was not even close to being his type. He must be more tired than he thought, it was addling his brain, impairing his ability to think properly. Still...Emma had felt it too, he was sure of it, the way her blue eyes widened, her soft gasp of surprise. Ivan had never had such an intense reaction to a single touch before, and it rattled his sense of equilibrium. A short laugh escaped Ivan as he suddenly pictured his mother, imagining what she would say if she knew he was lusting over someone like Emma. Ivan sighed up at the ceiling, admitting defeat, he rose to take a cold shower.

Emma had been determined not to worry, not to obsess over a possible impending pregnancy, but now, knowing that Ivan was here, in the same town, the same hospital as her, made that virtually impossible. Emma had tried to play it cool, had pretended that she couldn't care less about the new doctor, but as soon as she got to work the following night, she quizzed her colleagues for information. As far as they were able to tell, Ivan had taken a twelve-month contract at the hospital. Staff gossip said he was single, not that Emma cared, came from a wealthy family, was friends with the director of medical services at the hospital, and that he was a trauma surgeon. Apparently, he had requested a position here, for personal reasons. Emma could only imagine what those personal reasons were! She was not at all surprised to see him approaching the switchboard window shortly before midnight, in fact, she had been expecting him to appear all night.

"Do you work every night shift?" Ivan said by way of a greeting.

"Yes."

"An eight-hour shift?"

"Sixteen," Emma didn't elaborate. Ivan's eyebrows shot through the roof.

"Sixteen?! That's insane! Definitely not a good idea for someone who is possibly pregnant, or at the very least, someone who is trying to conceive."

"Is that why you have come here then, Ivan, to lecture me?" Emma rolled her eyes.

"If need be". Good grief, the man had no shame! "So," Ivan cleared his throat awkwardly, gesturing pointedly at Emma's stomach. "Are you? Pregnant I mean?"

"I don't know," Emma crossed her arms over her chest and fixed Ivan with a blunt stare. "It is too early to tell, but even if I did know, it would be none of your business!"

"Cut the crap Emma, we both know full well that it will be my business, whatever the outcome!"

"Is that why you requested this job?" Emma's eyes narrowed. "So that you could spy on me?" When Ivan didn't deny it, Emma continued. "You really are a piece of work Ivan Delgado; I'll give you that much." A spate of calls came in then, and Ivan, feeling very much as if he had just been quite literally saved by the bell, took his leave, deciding it was best to give Emma a chance to calm down and think things through rationally.

Emma couldn't believe the nerve of Ivan! How dare he waltz in here and start to tell her what she could and couldn't do, how dare he butt into her private business, Emma fumed. She wished she could forget all about him, but she couldn't. Not with his incessant night-time wandering of the switchboard corridor. Emma saw Ivan so much that she started to question if he really did have a job at the hospital after all, or if he was just lying to get close to her, to the possible baby. Emma wanted to know why he cared so much. If the hospital gossips were right, Ivan was not married. If he wanted kids so much, why didn't he have any already? Why had he donated his sperm in the first place? Emma wondered who the intended recipient was supposed to have been. A girlfriend perhaps? A fiancé? She found the thought that Ivan had someone special in his life oddly discomforting, a feeling she hastened to squash down. It was just a lack of sleep, Emma decided, and perhaps the irritation of the situation, that was all. Absolutely nothing else. Emma was not interested in Ivan Delgado at all, not even if he was the sexiest man she had ever met, which, she was forced to admit, he was. No, Emma reminded herself, she was not interested in Ivan Delgado at all. It would be something that she repeated to herself throughout the rest of her shift.

Emma had always thought of herself as pretty patient, but Ivan was testing even her to her limits. She had never met anyone as pig-headed as Ivan, of that she was sure. He just would not leave well enough alone. At first, it was her working hours he was berating her for, the next night it was her diet!

"Is that decaf?" Emma could feel Ivan's scowl from across the office.

"Nope," she popped the P, walking back to her desk with the offending cup of tea and taking a large swig in front of the switchboard window where Ivan currently stood frowning at her.

"You need to switch to decaf, it's not saf-" Ivan broke off, gaping at Emma. "You are not seriously going to eat that, are you?"

"Do you really have nothing better to do than to come down here and ruin my dinner?" Emma turned to look at Ivan, completely exasperated.

"You call that dinner?" Was she serious? He was not entirely sure what exactly that was that she was eating, but he was reasonably certain that it couldn't be called food. "It looks thoroughly revolting."

"No, Ivan," Emma threw her dinner in the rubbish bin, plate and all, having suddenly lost her appetite. "I guess not."

"So now you are not going to eat at all?" Appalled, Ivan knew he was the cause and scrambled to find something to say. "That isn't very wise either." Seriously? It isn't wise? Ivan gave himself a mental slap. He was supposed to be keeping an eye on Emma, that was all, not interfering! All he wanted to know was if she was pregnant or not, and if so, find a way to be involved. If he was being honest with himself, he also wanted to find out who she was dating, and hopefully give them a friendly warning about women like Emma.

Still, he was never going to get her to tell him anything if he kept acting like an arse.

"Sorry," his tone sounded gruff, even to his ears. Ivan was a man who was not used to having to say sorry. He lived his life on his terms, without apology. "I am sure you know what you are doing."

Ivan decided that he needed to back off. After last night's debacle over Emma's dinner choices, Ivan knew that he was pushing his luck. He couldn't afford to risk completely alienating Emma. Not until he knew for certain if she was in fact pregnant or not. Deciding a peace offering was the best course of action, Ivan found the website for a local florist and ordered her the most expensive bouquet they had. He had the feeling that Emma would not care about the cost of the flowers, but Ivan wanted to make a statement, he needed to make sure that Emma forgave him, and he was not above using the prettiest bunch of flowers money could buy to convince her! He knew the flowers had been delivered, he walked past the switchboard window during his shift and caught her admiring them, although he noticed that she had removed the card he had the florist include. It was probably just as well, there was no reason for the rest of her team to know who had sent her the flowers. As long as she forgave him, that was all that mattered. She gave him a tentative smile as he passed by, and a truce was formed.

"Why are you stalling?" Emma didn't even bother looking up to know it was Ivan at her switchboard window. Even if she didn't recognise his voice, like molten chocolate, he had taken to stopping by at the same time every night. Every. Single. Night. After two weeks, it really was most annoying and starting to drive Emma insane. She knew the security guards were starting to get suspicious of what exactly was going on between her and Ivan, they saw him here each time they left on their rounds. Emma knew it was only a matter of time before the rumour mill got started, which was the very last thing that she wanted.

"What?" Emma put down the roster she had been working on and gave Ivan her full attention.

"Why are you stalling? It has been a month since you were inseminated, have you gotten your period yet or not?" How on Earth did he know that it had been a month?

"Firstly, I am not stalling," Emma huffed, "and secondly, that is none of your business!" There was no way that Emma was going to talk to Ivan about her period, good heavens, how embarrassing!

"Emma," Ivan's voice was irritatingly placating. "We've been through this, I have a right to know, I want to know," Ivan was surprised to find that he actually meant what he had said, he really did want to know. "Please don't argue with me."

"Fine," Emma's tone softened, she was far too tired to argue with him anyway. "Ivan I really don't know yet, I promise. I have this weekend off; I was going to do the test once I got home on Friday morning." Emma would never admit it to Ivan, but she was nurturing a small hope. Her period was two days late, not really that unusual for her, but still, she was hopeful. She just wanted to wait until the weekend. She knew that if she was not pregnant, she would be too upset to come to work anyway and would need a couple of days to have a darn good cry.

"Good," Ivan nodded, "I will meet you; we will do the test together."

"What? No."

"Emma-"

"Ivan, no." Emma's voice held no room for argument. "I will do the test on Friday, by myself. I will call you once I know what the result is." A thought occurred to Emma. "You don't trust me to tell you the truth," she nodded in understanding. "We work together Ivan; it would be too hard to try and hide a pregnancy. In any case, I am happy to show you the test, or in that case, do a second test later with you present." It was not what Ivan was hoping to hear at all. Emma was right though; Ivan didn't trust her to tell him the truth. No, he would just have to come up with a foolproof plan to have her take the test in front of him.

Just before Emma's shift was due to finish on Friday morning, a hospital appointment reminder popped up in the corner of Emma's computer screen, making her jump. She didn't remember having an appointment, which was most unlike her, and she hastily scribbled the details down on a sticky note, attaching it to the front of her locker. The timing would be tight, even though the appointment was here at the hospital outpatients department, she would need to go directly from work to be there on time. Emma sighed, she had the beginnings of a headache, and had been looking forward to going straight home. She wanted three things; a nice hot shower, her comfortable bed, and twelve hours of uninterrupted sleep. Unfortunately for Emma, it didn't seem likely that she would be getting any of the three.

CHAPTER FOUR

"Emma Roberts." The nurse called her name just as she rounded the corner, and she hurried across to the reception desk. "The doctor is ready for you now," the nurse checked her chart. "He is in room 203, you can go straight in. Just head down this corridor, take the first right, and then it is the second door on the left." Emma found the consulting room without any issue and knocked loudly.

"Enter," Emma frowned, the muffled voice sounded all too familiar to her. She pushed the door open and stood there, dumbfounded. "Emma," Ivan stood in front of her, a sheepish look on his face. "You made it."

"I, what?" Emma gaped at him. "You tricked me? Why?" Emma thought they had a truce, but this only proved otherwise.

"Why? Emma, why do you think? I have waited over a month now to find out if you are in fact carrying my child. Enough waiting Emma. I have a right to know. I want to know, and I want to know now!"

"What the hell?!" Emma spat out, anger bubbling up inside her at Ivan's blatant manipulation. "You tried to manipulate me? You really are a piece of work, Ivan, do you know that?" Ignoring her outburst, Ivan took a specimen jar down from the shelf and held it out to Emma. "Are you serious right now?" When Ivan remained quiet, Emma snatched the jar from his hand

and threw it at him, hitting him squarely in the jaw, feeling rather satisfied with her aim.

Ivan was stunned. He had no idea that Emma was such a wildfire. He would have to watch out for that in the future, that was for sure. The unbidden thought rattled him. Wait, future? With Emma? No way! Never going to happen, even if she was his type, which, he looked her up and down, she most certainly was not. No, there was one reason and one reason only why he was interested in Emma, and that was solely because she was most likely carrying his child.

"Emma," Ivan retrieved a second specimen jar from off of the shelf, "please be reasonable. You were intending on doing the pregnancy test today anyway, at least this way we will both find out the result at the same time, it is only fair."

"Fair? Do you think this situation is fair? You booked me an appointment that I didn't need, or want, in order to trick me into doing a pregnancy test with you present, and you think this is fair? Is it fair that I should even be here in the first place? Is it fair that you are here? There was a reason that I opted for an anonymous donor Ivan, so that he would remain unknown. This is supposed to be my baby Ivan, not your baby, not our baby, mine. So, you tell me, what exactly is fair about this situation?"

"I am sorry that the mix up with the donor samples happened, truly, I am sorry that all of your well-laid plans have been messed up, but seriously, we are talking about a baby here, so put your personal life on hold for two minutes and take the damn test." This time when Ivan held the specimen jar out Emma took it.

"Fine." Emma dropped her bag on the gurney and stomped through to the adjoining bathroom to fill up the specimen jar.

Once she returned, she sat, arms crossed, at the desk opposite Ivan, watching as he performed the pregnancy test. She knew, before he uttered the words, she knew simply by the way his face paled, she knew.

"Emma," Ivan spoke softly, "you are pregnant." Overcome with a conflicting array of emotions, Emma bursts into tears. To be honest, it was not quite the reaction that Ivan was expecting from Emma. He genuinely thought that she had already known that she was pregnant, that she was simply holding out on him, but the way her eyes had rounded in surprise as the words had left his lips left him in no doubt. She had not known; she had been telling him the truth this entire time. Ivan was not quite sure how to feel about that, he was used to women being deceptive little creatures, using lies and tears to get their own way. Emma was a refreshing change to all of that. Ivan was starting to wonder if his earlier assumptions he had made about Emma were in fact accurate.

"Emma," Ivan crossed to her side, kneeling down next to her. "Please don't cry." Emma takes in a shaky breath and looks at Ivan for the first time.

"You can't tell me what to do Ivan, I don't care if this baby is biologically yours, it doesn't mean that you can tell me what to do."

"No, I suppose it doesn't," Ivan nodded thoughtfully. "We have a lot to discuss Emma, not now obviously, you need time to digest this news, we both do, but later, once we have had time to think, we will need to discuss how to move on from here."

"I won't agree to a termination, Ivan," Emma's arms wrapped protectively around her waist as if she was worried that Ivan was about to cart her off to theatre right then and there.

"What?" Ivan was genuinely surprised, he had no intention of even discussing a termination, disappointed that Emma would think so little of him as to believe that he was that type of a man. "Emma, no, never!" Ivan's tone was so firmly adamant that Emma didn't doubt him.

"Good," Emma's voice betrayed her with a wobble, her eyes tearing up again. She ducked her head so that Ivan would not see.

"Is that the only thing that is bothering you, Emma?" Ivan swallowed thickly.

Emma shook her head to try and clear her thoughts. How could she explain everything that she was feeling to Ivan? She was not sure that she could, or that she even wanted to. "This is a very small hospital; it won't be long until word will get out."

"Are you worried that people will talk, that the truth will come out?" Ivan understood completely. It would not be easy for Emma, that was for sure. Now that Ivan was in the picture, there was no chance of her passing her pregnancy off to her boyfriend as a happy surprise. Any chance of a marriage proposal from him was long gone. Ivan would like to say that he felt sorry about that, but truthfully, he didn't.

"Aren't you?! I can hear them all talking now, the nurses will wonder how I managed to snare you, the doctors will wonder why you allowed me to continue with the pregnancy, a possible career killer for you, and the admin staff will be beyond jealous that I was successful where they have previously failed." Emma sniffed loudly. "I don't even know anything about you," she lamented. "Oh no!" Emma suddenly lifted her head, the top of which nearly collided with Ivan's nose. "Are you married?" Emma squeaked. "Girlfriend? Fiancé? Partner?"

"No, Emma," Ivan was sombre. "I am single." Unlike you, the thought pops, unbidden, into his head.

Ivan finds himself strangely affected by Emma's display of vulnerability and yearns to comfort her. He has the strangest desire to pull her into his arms and simply hold her until her tears stop, a desire he deliberately resists. Instead, Ivan opts for words. "Emma, please don't cry. It will all work out; I promise you that." Even as Ivan speaks the words, he has no idea how they will ever be true. "I know this isn't entirely as you had planned this pregnancy to be, but I am sure we can all come to an understanding, one that is fair, to everyone involved. Come on," he helps her to her feet, "let me take you home." It was a testament to how rattled Emma was, that she let Ivan physically lead her out of the hospital, past a number of staff members, all too curious to bother hiding their speculative stares. Indeed, Emma didn't speak at all until they were in

Ivan's rental car, and even then, it was only to give him
her address.

CHAPTER FIVE

Ivan was not sure what he was expecting to see, but this certainly was not it. From the outside, Emma's house was nothing like Ivan had ever seen before, anywhere, and he had travelled extensively. He felt as if he were looking at some sort of storybook cottage, and half expected a barrage of woodland creatures to spring out from behind the fence, in a full song and dancc routine. Surrounded by a rickety fence that had clearly seen far better days, Emma's house was cute, Ivan decided, there really was no other word for it. Painted a sickening shade of pink, it was impossible to miss, sitting amongst a jungle of neglected plants and shrubs. Ivan wanted to ask her if she had chosen that colour herself, but one look at her face and he decided against it. Her front door was an ode to stained glass, and once inside, Ivan was relieved to discover that Emma's house was an oasis against the scorching heat outside.

Off the small entry was a spacious lounge room, which was furnished with a mismatched assortment of brightly coloured armchairs, soft cotton lounges, and a violent green velvet recliner. The walls were a brave shade of tangerine orange, and Ivan began to think that he was hallucinating. He had never seen so many different colours in the one place before, it made his head spin. A large distressed blue coffee table sat in the middle of a fuchsia rug, flanked by two oddly sculpted stained-glass lamps. There were large pillar candles and tubs of flowering cacti stacked haphazardly on the tabletop. Every single inch of available wall was taken up with bookcases, although that was clearly not enough, as there were also stacks of books piled in front of the bookcases. Emma was obviously a reader, an interesting discovery. Emma brushed past Ivan and flopped down on one of the sofas, utterly exhausted.

Seizing on the opportunity to have a gentle snoop around, Ivan offered to fetch Emma a glass of water, heading off in search of the kitchen in the direction Emma had indicated. Although small, Emma's house made up for its size by the creative use of the space. As Ivan walked down a short centre hallway, he felt like he was walking through a photo album, there were so many photographs up on the wall. He looked through them slowly, searching for clues. There were one or two photographs of Emma with another woman, a sister perhaps, and dozens of nature photographs, but absolutely none of them were of Emma and a man. In fact, what he had seen of the house so far was incredibly feminine. Returning with the water, Ivan sunk onto the sofa next to Emma, his weight dipping the middle of the sofa, causing her to slide towards him, only stopping once their thighs were pressing together.

"Emma," Ivan's voice was thick with emotion, and a desire he tried to ignore. It was just the proximity making him feel this way, that was all, he tried to convince himself. "Do you want me to call someone for you?

"No," she jerked her head, shook it as if dislodging a cobweb. They sat unmoving, silence stretching all around them, engulfing them, endless in all directions. Ivan scratched the back of his neck, uncomfortable. He was a world-renowned trauma surgeon for goodness sake, he was not used to such suffocating stillness crawling across his skin, making him itch.

"Why are there no photographs of your boyfriend on the walls?" His voice sounded loud, even to his own ears, slashing across the silence with a jarring edge.

"Who?" Emma shook her head to dispel the fogginess. She had barely heard anything else after Ivan had told her that she was pregnant. Her heart was singing, she felt like she was floating, such an intense happiness filled her every pore. Her dream was actually coming true, finally, finally, she was going to be a mother.

"Your boyfriend?" Ivan pushed, staring at her intently, obviously expecting an answer.

"Boyfriend?" It was Emma's turn to be confused. "I don't have a boyfriend."

"You don't what?" Ivan was stunned. Had he heard her correctly? If she didn't have a boyfriend, that would mean...Good grief! Ivan paled as realisation dawned on him. "Are you telling me that you are single?" He questioned quietly, his voice barely a whisper.

"Of course I am single," Emma stared at Ivan, her brows knitting together in a frown. "Why on Earth would I be using a sperm donor, or for that matter, going through In Vitro Fertilisation alone, if I had a boyfriend?"

"I just thought..." Ivan trailed off; he was not sure what to say. He felt like a fool. All this time he had misjudged her, simply presumed that she would be using a sperm donor in order to try and trap someone into marrying her. Yet here she was, as single as he was, choosing to head into motherhood alone. Why would she do that?

"Actually, you know what, don't bother trying to explain," Emma's eyes narrowed, "I can pretty much guess what you were thinking." There was no mistaking the acid in Emma's tone. Ivan felt suitably chastised, he had acted like a heel without any just cause. He had blown it, he realised uncomfortably, there would be no chance of an amicable relationship with Emma now, not even for the sake of their child.

"Emma, forgive me, please. I misjudged the situation." Ivan would not blame her if she never forgave him for his misjudgement of her, but he knew he had to try. "Can we start again? Try to be friends?" Silence. Ivan squirmed under Emma's relentless gaze, fervently wishing that she would say something, anything, instead of just sitting there, staring at him in suffocating silence.

"Fine," Emma broke the silence, she quite liked the thought of starting over, a new beginning to mark the new life growing within her seemed appropriate somehow. Besides, Ivan was a trauma surgeon, not an axe murderer, being friends with him was harmless enough, was not it? If he was going to insist on having a role in her child's life, she owed it to herself to at least be civil.

"Hi," she wriggled her entire body around to face him straight on, holding her hand out towards him. "I'm Emma," she smiled at him, "I'm single, newly pregnant, and a lover of bad reality television shows. It is nice to meet you."

"I'm Ivan", he smiled widely, a warmth coursing throughout his body. "I'm single, a newly expectant father, and a lover of lazy Saturdays. It is nice to meet you." He took her outstretched hand in his and shook it slowly, reluctant to release it. He felt a shift and wondered if Emma could sense it too. She was single, his head was spinning. He had so many questions, he wondered if he dared ask her. Why was she wanting to be a single mother? Why was not she in a relationship? It was not as if she was a horrid person, far from it. All of the hospital gossip that Ivan had heard about Emma had been positive, everyone seemed to say the same things. She was a hard worker, generous with her praise, always happy to go out of her way to help others. Ivan had also managed to discover that Emma was quite the crusader, spending most of her spare time fighting to make a difference in the lives of those less fortunate than herself. How could he have been so very wrong about her?

Emma swallowed the lump in her throat and clenched her jaw tightly shut, refusing to allow it to gape open as it wanted to at the sight of Ivan watching her with those brooding brown eyes of his. She could get lost in his eyes, a thought which both surprised and scared her. She was not one to trust easily, and unlike her sister, Emma didn't have a wealth of dating experience to draw upon. Still...Her eyes lingered on Ivan's navy coloured tee pulled tightly across his chest, showcasing his well-defined chest, before travelling over his face and up to his hair. Good lord, he was gorgeous! His olive skin was tantalising, hinting at his European heritage, Spanish maybe? Emma's fingers itched to run through his chestnut brown hair that he wore in a spiky fashion. His jaw was strong, chiselled, with the hint of a dimple at the edge of his luscious, full lips. Emma wondered what they would be like to taste. Sweet, she decided, like honey, but with a hint of saltiness. Emma let her eyes travel down, across his chest, wondering if it felt as hard as it looked. Enough! Emma scolded herself mentally, mortified as a blush slowly crept up her pale face. Don't you dare look at him that way, her internal monologue continued, there is no way he is your type! Emma sighed regretfully, she hated it when her inner voice was right, which was usually always.

Ivan couldn't breathe. He wondered if Emma knew how she was looking at him, as if she wanted to devour him. What was she seeing? Did he pass her appraisal? Ivan was not willing to analyse just why right now, but it was suddenly vital that he passed her appraisal. He wanted her to be pleased with him, as arrogant as that sounded. Perhaps it was a primal thing, harking back from caveman days? They were having a baby together after all, even if they didn't get any of the fun of making said baby. Ivan grew uncomfortably tight at the thought, glad of the fact that he was wearing his scrubs. At least they were looser than his jeans. Emma knew that she should move her eyes, look away, look anywhere but at Ivan, but she couldn't tear her eyes away. Traitors that they were, they just dipped lower and lower, taking in every single inch of him. She could see his taut thighs straining against the fabric of his blue hospital scrubs, her mouth going dry at the thought of what lay beneath, good grief, what she would not give to have her sister's confidence right now.

Aching, itching to reach out and touch him, Emma curled her treacherous fingers into a ball and squashed them in between her knees. A staged cough from Ivan jerked Emma out of her reverie and brought her back to her senses. She looked up, directly into his amused eyes.

"See anything you like?" Ivan teased. Seeing the way Emma blushed a deep shade of crimson, Ivan decided that she had definitely found something she liked, which was a very interesting thought indeed. Without overthinking it, Ivan closed the distance between him and Emma, cupped her face gently in his hands, and slowly lowered his face to hers, kissing her. Emma gasped with surprise as Ivan's lips pressed against hers, her lips parting involuntarily, heat pooling in between her thighs, dampening the scrap of silk she wore underneath her dress.

Emma had never before experienced such a powerful reaction to a kiss, and she linked her hands together behind his head, urging him closer. Ivan's tongue nudged her lips, seeking, and being granted, access. His tongue was silk, Emma decided, as it danced with hers, duelling for dominance, probing her mouth, tasting and sucking. His hands moved to her back, drawing her closer to his chest, angling her head in order to deepen the kiss. Sliding her fingers through his luscious hair, Emma pressed his mouth closer still, arching her back against him and groaning into the kiss, feeling him smile as she did so. She was on fire, every inch of her skin burning, aching to be touched by his hands. In a faraway part of her brain, Emma was vaguely away that she had moved, that she now straddled Ivan's lap, but she couldn't find the sense to care.

Ivan ached to taste her, to sample every single inch of Emma. To fill her up until she screamed his name in rapture, to watch her eyelids grow heavy with desire, as he knew they would. Her scent filled his nostrils and clouded his senses. He wanted her, he lusted for her. She lusted after him too, his mind crowed triumphantly. Ivan knew it, Emma wanted him. The very thought brought him up cold and he reluctantly forced himself to end the kiss. It was not right, lust or not, taking Emma like this, while she was pregnant, was not the right thing to do. No, he had to set the ground rules, before lines got blurred and emotions became involved. Emma shook her head, momentarily disorientated.

"Emma," Ivan started, "That was-"

"A mistake, I know, I'm sorry", Emma gasped out hastily, cutting Ivan off midsentence, clumsily scrambling off of his lap and regaining her footing on the floor, her face beet red, eyes fixed firmly on the floor.

"Really?" Ivan cocked an eyebrow, surprise lacing his words. "You think so?"

"Yes, of course," Emma stated emphatically, her voice a mortifying squeak. "Don't you?" She fought to steady her breathing, vaguely wondering why he was not short of breath as well, was he that unaffected by their shared kiss? Or, worse still, had she been that dreadful a kisser? She wanted the floor to open up and swallow her whole, she had never been more embarrassed in all her life. "I mean, we don't even know each other, you work at the same small hospital as I do, obviously, this is a very small town." Emma was aware that Ivan was looking at her strangely, that she was babbling like a crazed fool, but was unable to stop herself, "and even if that was not the case, you are a doctor and I'm not, anyway, I am not looking for a relationship," she finished in a rush, not at all truthful.

"I think that was intoxicating Emma," Ivan countered, wondering just why it was that she was acting like a shy teenager. "I stopped so that we could lay some ground rules, so that there are no regrets later, nothing to impact the two of us parenting our child amicably," Ivan stood, closing the space between him and Emma in a single stride.

"We are two consenting adults Emma, who are obviously attracted to each other, and I would like to continue this...," he trailed off, dipping his head to feather kisses along Emma's jawline and down her slender neck, "at a later time." Ivan stepped back, capturing Emma's hand as he did, a hungry look clouding his eyes as his gaze raked over Emma's supple body, a groan escaping at the sight of her breasts, her nipples visibly hard beneath her shirt. "We've both had an emotional day, we need time to think, to sort out our plans going forward," his lips brushed her hand, "I'll go, I left my number on the memo pad on the fridge, if you need me, call." Long after Ivan had gone, Emma could still feel his touch, her skin was molten, branded from where his hands had been. She knew she was in trouble. If he could incite such a reaction from her with a single kiss, how on earth was she ever going to accept anything less? She had just condemned herself to a lifetime of celibacy, she was certain of it. There was no doubt in Emma's mind that there was not another single person alive who would be able to match Ivan's kisses, or more worryingly, her reaction to them. What on Earth was she going to do now?

CHAPTER SIX

She was going to throttle him, that is what she was going to do, Emma decided at some point near midnight when she took yet another telephone call from Ivan, the fifth in this shift alone.

"Switchboard."

"Emma, it's me."

"Yes doctor," Emma tried not to groan at the sound of Ivan's voice, glancing at the computer to see that he was, in fact, calling from the doctor's residence, and not from theatres.

"You know you really should call me Ivan," his voice was teasing, but Emma was not in the mood.

"I'm about to head home, what did you need?"

"Do you want me to drive home with you, follow you in my car I mean, to make sure you get home safely?"

"What? No, why on earth would I want that?"

"I just thought, what with the baby and all..." Ivan trailed off.

"You thought what? That suddenly the town would be full of dark and dangerous monsters all trying to get me? Seriously, Ivan, go to bed." Emma hung up with a click, hoping her annoyance kept him up all night.

It had been six days since Emma had found out that she was pregnant. Six long, never-ending days. Already it had felt to Emma as if she had been pregnant for six months instead of just six days, a fact that had absolutely nothing to do with her or her pregnancy, and instead had everything to do with Ivan. He had been insufferable, and secretly Emma wished that he didn't know, that he never needed to know about her baby. She knew that genetically, he was the baby's father, but as far as she was concerned, that didn't give him free rein over her life. She stretched her arm out from under the warmth of the bed covers to retrieve her vibrating mobile from the bedside table, growling at the sight of Ivan's name flashing on the screen, before pitching her telephone across the room, smiling at the satisfying sound it made when it hit the bedroom wall. Seriously, she shook her head, all she wanted was a day, maybe two, where Ivan didn't annoy her incessantly. Was that really too much to ask?

It was no surprise to Emma that Ivan was waiting for her when she arrived at work that night, annoying looking as sexy as hell, a dangerous glint in his eyes.

"Doctor," Emma nodded curtly, ignoring how his eyes narrowed at her use of his title instead of his name. Well, tough, let him stew. There was no way she was going to call him Ivan at work, not with her nosey co-workers around, that was for sure! The last thing, the very last thing, that Emma wanted was for rumours to get started, especially before she started to show her pregnancy. She didn't need people guessing that Ivan was the baby's father, even if they were right, she didn't need to be gossiped about. She needed to keep this job, more so now that there was a baby on the way. She smiled to herself as she logged in to the computer system and got herself set up for her shift. She knew it was early, maybe too early, but if she had a spare moment tonight, she wanted to try and have a look on the internet at pregnancy and baby-related stuff. She hoped to start a baby wishlist at all of the major retail stores, and then compare the prices to see who was cheaper. That way she could have a visual checklist of everything that she needed to buy as well as everything that she had already bought for her little one.

The first twenty minutes of her shift flew past, and Emma was surprised to see Ivan still standing at the switchboard window when she looked up again.

"Doctor," Emma gasped, "I'm sorry, did you need something?"

"What are you doing for dinner tonight?" Ivan spoke in an undertone, conscious of other staff members still milling around.

"Dinner?" Emma's eyebrows knitted together. "Are you serious right now?"

"I've never been more serious," Ivan slid a covered tray through the window, "here, I had the kitchen make you something."

"Excuse me?!".

"It's a perfect meal really, full of the nutrients and vitamins that you need right now."

"How the hell would you know what it is that I need right now?"

"I'm a doctor, Emma," Ivan stated as if it should be an obvious conclusion.

"Yes, doctor," Emma gleefully exaggerated the word, "I'm well aware of that, but the thing is, you are not my doctor, so thank you, but no thank you," Emma turned from the window, ignoring the tray.

"Emma, don't be silly," Ivan started, "you need to eat."

"And I will," Emma gestured to the bright pink lunch bag sitting on the counter behind her, "and before you ask," Emma held up a finger to silence Ivan, "a cheese sandwich and some strawberries." She decided it was best not to mention that her lunch bag also contained a can of soda and some biscuits.

"That's fine if you weren't pregnant," Emma shushed him loudly, convinced half the hospital had heard him, "but you are, with my child if I might remind you, and therefore, you need to eat healthy Emma, which is what this is." Ivan pushed the tray a little bit further through the window.

"What the hell?!" Emma hissed, standing and taking the tray, dumping the entire thing in the rubbish bin. "Let's get one thing straight right now. You do not get to tell me what I can or cannot do, is that understood? Also, since we seem to be discussing it now, instead of at a more convenient time," she glared at Ivan, "this is not your baby or our baby, it is my baby. You are a genetic error, that is all, nothing more than a clinical one night stand, and you can try to bully me if you like, but I think that if I got my own lawyer they would tell me that I don't have to tell you anything to do with my pregnancy, I don't have to share with you full stop. We are not in a relationship, I don't owe you anything,"

Emma spat out, beyond livid. "I don't know who the hell you think you are, but calling me several times a day, wanting to know how much sleep I have or have not had, needing to know how many calories I have or have not consumed, bringing me healthy food because you seem to think that as a doctor you know better than I do what is or is not good for me right now, is just plain meddling! And another thing," Emma continued, "I am not some sort of rent a womb, I am not having this baby for you. You do understand that, right Ivan? We are not making some sort of weird family unit here".

After his dressing down from Emma, Ivan had not slept well. In fact, he had spent most of the night tossing and turning, wondering if she had meant what she had said, and worse still, wondering if it was true. He was more than a clinical one night stand, was not he? At least as far as the courts were concerned? By the time the sun's rays were finally starting to spread over the horizon, Ivan knew what he was going to do.

"Listen, John, I just want to make sure that the child, my child, is looked after, and that he, or she, knows who their father is." Ivan drummed his lean fingers impatiently on his desk, frustrated with the turn his telephone call had taken. "John, look, I know you are only trying to help, but I don't need counselling or mediation, or any other such thing, seriously. Emma and I are fine, this custody agreement is merely a formality, a backup plan. I want to make sure that we are all covered and taken care of should something

49

unforeseen happen. I want to pre-empt any battles further down the line."

"Ivan, you are one of my oldest friends. Can I give you a piece of advice?"

"You are going to anyway, aren't you?"

"Yes," John stated, both friends chuckling, knowing each other all too well. "Seriously Ivan, you are not your father, you don't have to act like you are."

The advice stung, which Ivan suspected was John's intent. Both sons of highly regarded doctors, Ivan and John were raised in privileged circumstances. They had wanted for nothing, nothing that is except a father. Both Ivan and John's fathers had worked twenty-hour days, rising to the top of their fields by their mid-thirties. Ivan had often marvelled at the fact his parents had ever found the time to even fall pregnant in the first place. He was raised knowing that his father loved him and provided for him, but without any emotional connection to those facts. Perhaps that was why both he and John had chosen careers where people trumped money, John a pro bono lawyer, and he a trauma surgeon at home among the poorest countries in the world.

"I am not acting like my father," Ivan spat out through clenched teeth.

"Really, Ivan?" John challenged his friend. "Have you spoken to Emma? Have you discussed drawing up a custody agreement? Did you talk about how this would look? How much time each party gets with the child? Who gets what holiday and how often?" At his friend's silence, John continued. "What about finances, has that come up? Ivan, all I am saying is that you need to think, really think, about what it is you are doing. This is not a child that was conceived through an act of love. Have you asked Emma why she chose to use In Vitro Fertilization? She didn't choose you to be her baby's father, Ivan, you know that. The fact that this child is genetically yours is nothing more than an oversight, a clinical error. Drawing up a custody agreement is one thing, but Ivan, if this were ever to go to court, it would not be a simple win for you. If you want my opinion, I suggest that you add the baby to your will, Emma too if you are so inclined, and then you take every day as it comes. Be thankful that Emma is even involving you, Ivan."

"Will you draw up the agreement or not?" Ivan snapped, massaging his temples in an attempt to disperse the migraine starting to brew there. He was not his father, he reminded himself, choosing to ignore John's advice about discussing anything with Emma. He was doing this for her baby, their baby, surely she would see that?

"Yes Ivan," John sighed deeply, his concern evident. "I will draw it up for you, as your friend. If you would like to tell me now what you want to be included, I can have something put together for you later today."

"Thank you. I guess I want all of the important stuff to be included," Ivan started. "I want both parties to always have a current address of where the other party resides, and I want to be able to contact the child by telephone, whenever I choose. Grandparents and extended family, on both sides, should be able to contact the child by telephone whenever they choose to for that matter. We will trade off Christmas, Easter, birthdays, and school holidays, whenever practical. Except for the big birthdays, those will be a shared celebration".

"Also," Ivan continued, "no party will take the child overseas without the consent of the other party, and both parties are to be contacted in case of any medical issues or emergencies. As far as finances, I will pay for all schooling costs, and we will both decide what school they attend. I will also pay all medical and dental bills and any costs associated with them coming to visit me. I will also pay child support to Emma, which she can use as she sees fit. I was thinking one thousand dollars a week."

"Ivan," John's tone was incredulous, "that is very generous, are you sure that you want to commit to that much?"

"Why not," Ivan shrugged his shoulders. "The money is just sitting there, goodness knows I don't use it, my child should be able to benefit from me financially. Besides," Ivan cleared his throat self-consciously, "it will mean that Emma is able to stay home with the child, and I know that she wants that opportunity."

A vision of Emma, propped up on her sofa, breastfeeding their child, a look of rapture etched onto her face sprung uninvited into Ivan's mind, quickly followed by one of Emma chasing after a dark-skinned toddler, warmth and joy radiating from their faces. Image after image played through Ivan's mind, like a movie, each one featuring Emma and a dark-skinned child. She was so gorgeous, he admitted to himself, his trousers becoming uncomfortable as he grew hard at the thought of Emma pregnant with his child, her stomach slowly swelling with his seed, her breasts growing heavy. He wondered how it would feel, how she would taste, his tongue darting across his lips in anticipation, longing to enclose his mouth over her hardened nipple. It took all his willpower not to moan out loud, a mortifying thought with John on the other end of the telephone.

"Ivan?"
"What?!" Ivan all but yelped, feeling rather like a teenager who had been sprung smoking by his parents.
"Did you hear what I said?"
"Oh, yes, I heard what you said."
"Well?"
"Well, what?"
"Ivan," John started, speaking to Ivan as one would speak to a child, "I was saying that if you give me Emma's address, I can send a copy directly to her if you would prefer?" Ivan rattled off Emma's address, shaking his head to clear the last of his visions of Emma.
"Thanks, John, I really appreciate this." Ivan terminated the call.

Ivan knew that he could trust John above anyone else in his life and felt oddly lighter than he had in a long time, it had been a wise move, calling John, and explaining the whole baby situation to him. John would have the custody agreement all drawn up by lunch and in the mail to Ivan and Emma this afternoon. This time next week everyone would know where they stood, and they could focus on what was really important, the baby, his baby, their baby. Ivan smiled as he completed his hospital rounds, not even last-minute shift changes or one of his interns dropping an entire tray of sterilized instruments on his foot could dampen his mood today, not now that he had his child's future secured.

Emma spotted Ivan on her way out of the hospital, and although he looked as if he was making a beeline for her, she ignored him, scampering to her car, and the safety of home. It had been a week since their altercation at the switchboard, and remarkably, he had left her alone, something that she despaired would ever happen. Pulling into her driveway, she collected her mail from the letterbox, letting herself into the house and throwing the stack of mail on the bench, along with her keys, turning to switch on the kettle. She glanced at the letters as she sat on one of the kitchen chairs, massaging her feet as she waited for the kettle to reach its crescendo. A heavy cream envelope peeked out at her from beneath a pile of advertising flyers and what she suspected were bills. Reaching over she fingered the envelope carefully, it was smooth, luxuriously so, it almost felt as if the envelope were made from some type of fabric rather than from paper.

Ripping it open she slid the contents from the envelope, her face losing all colour as she skimmed the letter. She was vaguely aware of someone knocking at her door, slipping through the house in a daze to answer it, Ivan standing on her doorstep.

"You." She spat out, voice shaking with anger.

"Emma," Ivan spotted the letter clutched in her hand, "let me explain."

"Get off my property! What the hell is wrong with you? I can't even start to understand you," Emma was aware that she was shouting now, really shouting, but was unable to stop herself. "You consulted a lawyer, without speaking to me first?! Why would you do that? How could you?!"

"Emma, it was the right thing to do," Ivan was cut off in his explanation.

"The right thing? No, Ivan, it was not the right thing to do," Emma fixes him with a cold hard stare. "You are not to contact me again, is that clear? Come near me again, at home or at work, and I will call the police. I do not want to hear from you, or see you, ever again, do you understand." She slams the door in his face, slumping to the floor, tears pouring down her face. What was she going to do? He couldn't take her baby, could he?

CHAPTER SEVEN

There, she had done it. Emma had finally told someone that she was pregnant. To be fair, it was her general doctor, but still, someone other than Ivan knew that she was having a baby, and unlike Ivan, Emma's doctor was thrilled for her, he knew how much Emma had wanted this. Emma had tried to act cool when she had walked into the doctor's room, had tried to act natural, but the moment her doctor had sat down opposite her, Emma had blurted out her news, and then promptly burst into tears! Her doctor had run a few tests, and given Emma an estimated due date, fairly simple to predict in this case as Emma knew the exact second that she had been inseminated. Emma had been plied with brochures and information and presented with her very own pregnancy bag; a sample bag provided to all expectant mothers. He had also given Emma a sample packet of anti-nausea medication, just in case, which Emma had smiled at and thrown into the bottom of her bag. She was as fit as a fiddle; she would not need those.

Two days later, she realised just how very wrong she had been. Emma rested her cheek on the cold tile of the bathroom floor, grateful that for now at least, the room had stopped spinning. How long she laid there she didn't know; time had lost all importance. Her life now revolved around a schedule of napping, sipping ginger ale, and being sick. Emma had never thrown up so much in all of her life, and it had started to take its toll. She was unable to avoid it at work and had been sent home, assuring her boss it was most likely just a virus. Emma had been forced to take two days off work, and then had her two days of rostered leave. She was supposed to be back at work tomorrow, although she had no idea how that was going to be possible, failing some miracle.

There was no way that she would tell them that she was pregnant, yet without a medical certificate, she would be forced to take leave without pay, not only a blow to her bank account, but that in itself would be cause enough for staff gossip, confidential or not. Her co-workers always had a way of finding out various tidbits of gossip to spread around like wildfire. She had booked in to see her regular doctor after lunch today, she just had to get there without being ill. If only the floor didn't feel so very cool and welcoming against her fevered skin.

By the time Emma woke it was pitch dark. Momentarily disorientated she stumbled around the room trying to find the light switch before flicking it on and flooding the room in light. Urgh, she was so parched! Emma flicked on lights as she walked through the house to the kitchen, stunned to see the numbers on the microwave reading two o'clock in the morning. She had slept the clock around. And, she grimaced, missed her appointment. Sipping her water slowly,

Emma realised that she was ravenous, and wondered if she dared try to eat anything. A rummage in her fridge produced a bowl of leftover braised steak and mashed potatoes, a quick zap in the microwave warmed it through nicely. Retrieving a fork from the top drawer Emma cautiously speared a piece of steak and popped it into her mouth, chewing slowly, deliberately, carefully looking for signs of nausea. Nothing. Delighted, Emma finished off her meal, glad to finally be feeling like her old self again. She tidied up the kitchen, snuggling down in bed with the television remote control, drifting off to sleep halfway through a rerun of her favourite sitcom.

Morning arrived with a vengeance, a tidal wave of nausea sending Emma scurrying for the sanctuary of the bathroom. Every time she moved, wave after wave of nausea would wash over her, she was either too hot or too cold, even the anti-nausea medication her general doctor had given her didn't work, they had merely come back up. She was a sick, smelly, teary, stressed mess, and, to top it all off, she had to call her boss and explain that she was ill and unable to get to a doctor for a medical certificate. If only there was some kind of doctor call out service or a doctor who did house calls. The more Emma mulled it over the more an idea started to form. It would not hurt to ask, would it? After all, he was a doctor, and he had said that he wanted to help her. Yet she had turned him away the last time he had been here, she had yelled at him and sent him away without a second thought, without giving him time to explain. He had said that he had been helping the baby and she had refused to listen. Maybe he would not want to help her now, Emma gnawed on her bottom lip, debating her options. They were limited. Call work without a medical certificate and take leave without pay, assuming that her boss even approved it, or call Ivan and ask him to write her a medical certificate.

With shaking fingers, she dialled a familiar number, dread pooling in her stomach.

"Delgado." He answered on the second ring, all businesslike and brisque.

"Ivan?" Her voice is barely a whisper.

"Emma?" His tone is guarded, detached. If he was surprised to hear from her, he didn't show it.

"Ivan, I'm sorry, I didn't know who else to call," Emma sniffs loudly, determined not to succumb to tears over the telephone, certainly not in front of Ivan in any case.

"Emma, are you crying? What's wrong?" Worry tinged his tone, and Emma felt wretched for calling him.

"I'm sorry, I shouldn't have called you, you have better things to do, I was being silly anyway, I'm sorry." Emma hung up the telephone and sank back against her pillows. Great, she scolded herself, now he probably thought she was needy and melodramatic, just the fuel he needed to show the courts that she was unfit to be a mother. The thought chilled her to the bone and set off another flood of tears, gasping sobs wrenching her body.

Her head was pounding, and it was getting louder. Emma lifted a groggy head off her damp pillows and strains to listen. There is it again, the banging. Urgh, someone was at the door, great, this what just what she needed on a day like today. She padded down the hall and cracked the door open a smidge, determined to tell whoever was banging to go away. Her blue eyes clashed with brown and gold flecks as she took in the sight of Ivan standing on her doorstep, brows furrowed. She let the door fall open, too happy to see him to care what she must look like.

"Emma, what on earth?" He gestured to her general appearance with a sweep of his hand. "What happened? Are you all right? Is it the baby?" His face paled and he gripped Emma's arms, his lean fingers digging into her elbows.

"No, it's not the baby, the baby is fine," Emma brushed his hands away, "that's all you care about, isn't it? It's me, Ivan, I'm si-si-sick." Emma finished on a sob, turning back into her house, not caring if he followed her or not at this point.

"Emma, wait, I'm sorry." Ivan stopped her as she reached her bedroom. "Let me look at you." His cool fingers felt Emma's forehead, checking for a temperature, she didn't even try to stop the moan from escaping past her lips at his touch.

"Mmm, you feel so nice," she turned her face into his hand. "Don't move, okay? Just stay there."

"Emma," Ivan pulled his hand away slowly, "that's not a good idea," he pushed her gently down until she was sitting on the side of the bed. "Come on, into bed with you."

"What? Now?!" Emma all but squealed, scrambling back onto the bed and tucking her legs under the covers.

"Yes now," Ivan raised a brow quizzically at her. "You are sick, bed is the best place to be right now.

"Oh. Right. Of course." Emma muttered, colour flooding her face.

"Interesting. What did you think I meant?" There was a teasing glint to Ivan's eyes.

"Nothing, nothing at all." Emma turned her face away from Ivan's gaze, heaven forbid he should see more in her expression than she wanted him to.

"Tell me what happened," Ivan sat down on the bed next to Emma, his thigh brushing ever so close to hers, taking her outstretched hand and placing his fingers on her pulse points.

"Morning sickness, although why they call it morning sickness, I have no idea, it is more like all day sickness," she gave Ivan a wry smile. "I can't keep anything down, I can't sleep, I can't work. Ivan, I, ah," Emma cleared her throat self-consciously, "I need a medicate certificate or my boss won't approve me taking off another day."

"Another one? How long have you been off work?"

"Four days." His eyebrows rose at her answer, but he said nothing.

"Be a good patient and stay put, I'll be back in a minute." Ivan strolled out down the hall, Emma could hear the sound of water running and drawers being opened and closed.

Ivan finally returned, bearing a tray laden with tea and dry toast. He had removed his jacket at some point, the sleeves of his crisp white shirt were rolled up to his elbows, showing off his olive complexion. Propping Emma up with pillows, he presented her with two tablets and a glass of water, which she took without question.

"Why didn't you tell me earlier that you were sick?" His question caught her off-guard. "Why go see another doctor, and presumably inform them of your pregnancy, why not come straight to me? I found a bottle of anti-nausea medication from last week." He held up the bottle as if expecting her to deny it.

"I was angry at you," Emma stared down at her comforter, tracing the intricate geometric patterns with her index finger. "You don't get to tell me what to do, you don't own me, Ivan."

"I know, I'm sorry. Honestly, Emma, I'm surprised you called me at all, especially considering how our last encounter ended."

"Well, you were quite the jerk," Emma offered him a wan smile.

"I can see that now, I guess I just wanted to do the right thing. I meant what I said the first day I met you, Emma. No child of mine will grow up without their father. I expect to be involved every step of the way, regardless of what happens in the future, this baby," Ivan tentatively reaches out and strokes Emma's still flat stomach, "our baby, will know me as his or her father."

"I was not expecting this, obviously, I had it all planned out, my little life, just me and my baby. I never expected to ever share it with someone," Emma confessed softly.

"Really," Ivan sounded surprised, "not ever, not even with a future husband?"

"Oh, for heaven's sake Ivan! Why are you so fixated on me having a boyfriend or husband or whatever?" Emma mutters as she pounds her pillow into submission, gratefully laying her head against the coolness of the pillowcase. "I already told you, I am single."

"I know, but-" Ivan was cut off by Emma interrupting.

"And not just newly single after breaking up with some hot stud of a boyfriend either. I am proper single, as in always single, perpetually single, as in never actually had a real boyfriend, or any kind of boyfriend actually, at all, ever."

"Are you serious right now?!" Ivan sounded incredulous. "Are you actually saying that you have never had a boyfriend, ever? How can that be? You are stunning!" His last comment earned a snort from Emma, along with an eye roll. "I'm serious Emma, I honestly cannot believe that some lucky guy hasn't scooped you up already."

"Well, thank you," Emma squirmed under Ivan's frank gaze. "In any case, I'm thirty-five years old Ivan,

I didn't want to wait. I have the means to support a child, the love, the financial security, so I decided to undergo In Vitro Fertilization. It is all I have ever wanted, to be a mama, nothing else matters." Emma ended on a sob, suddenly overwhelmed with emotions.

"Emma," Ivan brushes a strand of hair away from her eyes, "it's going to be okay."

"I know, I am just so happy."

"Emma," Ivan's tone was serious, "can you please forgive me? Or can you at least try to forgive me? I, my father, well, he was never around when I was a child. Please, Emma, I don't want that to be me, no matter how our child came to be, please, I'm begging you, Emma, please let me be involved. I promise not to overstep," at Emma's indelicate snort Ivan amended his choice of words, "much. I'll take your lead, please Emma, I just want to be involved."

"It won't be easy Ivan," Emma warned, "I'm used to being on my own, I'm not used to having someone to confide in, it might take me a while to get used to that. Also, sometimes," she leaned forward as whispered in a conspiratorial voice, "I can be a little bit bossy." At this Ivan tossed back his head, a bark of laughter escaping his perfectly formed mouth.

"I'll take my chances," he assures her with a wicked grin.

"In that case," Emma extends her hand, "a truce." Ivan takes her hand and shakes.

"Oh, and Emma, just so you know," he leans close enough to whisper in her ear, his warm breath sending shivers down her spine, "if you weren't so sick, I would have you in this bed, your legs wrapped tightly around me, screaming my name." Mouth dry, all Emma could do was gape at Ivan as he winked at her and tucked her up in bed, whistling to himself.

CHAPTER EIGHT

Within a few days, Emma was back to her normal, bubbly self, gladly putting the morning sickness behind her. Ivan warned her not to get too carried away, that she was still within the first trimester and therefore could experience more episodes of morning sickness, but for now, Emma was optimistic. They had agreed not to inform anybody of her pregnancy until she started showing, and only then would they tell their families. Emma would submit a request for maternity leave shortly after that, hating the thought of all of the nosey stares and questions. Ivan had tried to reassure her, but he knew that she was right, when the time came, she would be bombarded with awkward questions. For now, though, they were in a state of comfort.

It had been surprisingly easy to fall into sync with Emma. On the days where their shifts mirrored each other's, they would head to Emma's after work for coffee or a meal. Ivan set about taming her jungle garden, Emma sat in the shade and watched him, occasionally asking him a question, or adding another item to her ever-growing list of things she would need to look at or buy or read up on before the baby arrived. It was on one such afternoon when Ivan stopped her midsentence and said "Emma, will you come to Brisbane with me?"

"Brisbane? Why?"

"I want you to meet my parents, I would like for them to at least think that we dated before announcing your pregnancy."

"Meet your parents huh?"

"You don't want to?"

"No, it isn't that," Emma tried to explain, "it's just that I have never met anyone's parents before, what if they don't like me?"

"Trust me, they'll love you, and anyway, if they don't, they are way too polite to ever say anything." The comment didn't make Emma feel any better.

"Okay," she nodded slowly, absently chewing the end of her pen, mulling it over, "let's go to Brisbane. When did you want to do this?"

"Soon, the next month or so," Ivan replied without hesitation.

"Okay, I'll check my roster and put in for leave." Emma flipped the page of her notebook over to start a new list, everything that she would need to do or buy before going to Brisbane with Ivan.

Nine days later Emma was sitting rigid in her business class seat, hyperventilating, tears streaking down her face, nails digging into her palms, hoping with every fibre of her being that the plane would come out of its climb safely, completely unaware of Ivan watching her, a look of horror and concern etched across his face.

"I'll be fine," she gasped as the plane suddenly banked across the clear azure sky, "I don't like flying." She felt a weight settle over her hand, looked down to see Ivan's hand on top of hers, his thumb slowly circling her knuckles, calming, reassuring. Once the seat belt sign was turned off Emma turned to Ivan, mortifyingly aware of how she must have looked to him.

"See, I'm fine now," she tried to make light of the situation.

"Does that happen every time you fly?"

"Yes."

"Then why fly?"

"I have places to go."

"You have places to go," Ivan parroted back, shaking his head. "You amaze me, Emma, you really do."

Emma watched as Ivan conversed with the flight attendant with ease, he oozed authority and charm, this man sitting beside her was most definitely used to the finer things in life.

"I was right," she stated simply.

"About?" Ivan prompted.

"You. You always travel business class, don't you, I can tell."

"Sometimes I travel first class," Ivan grinned.

"Huh!" Emma snorted. "It figures." She sat quietly for a moment. "How do you stand it? Don't you feel like you are on display, like you are in a fishbowl?

"It doesn't bother me," Ivan shrugged. "You don't like being noticed, do you, Emma?"

"No, it makes me feel self-conscious and foolish. I prefer to be in the background."

"You could never be in the background, even if you tried," Ivan replied softly, turning back to his laptop propped open on the tray in front of him. it was not until lunch was served that Emma realised that Ivan still held her hand captive, a light blush colouring her cheeks as she realised that she didn't mind at all, in fact, she quite liked the feel of his hand touching her.

The flight landed without incident, Emma thankfully managed to keep most of her composure on landing, Ivan watching her like a hawk. Business-class had its perks, Emma decided, as they disembarked swiftly, Emma all but sprinting to the closest restroom. Emma's breath hitched as she caught sight of Ivan, casually leaning against the wall opposite the bathroom, eyes hooded, waiting for her. Hormones, she reminded herself sternly, that is all it was. Once they had retrieved their luggage, Ivan surprised Emma by leading her towards the parking garage instead of towards the taxi rank.

"Seriously?" She quirked an eyebrow at him as he drew her to a stop beside a metallic blue convertible. "This is what you drive? Has it been parked here the whole time you've been away?"

"No," Ivan stowed their luggage before coming around to open the car door for her, waiting for her to slide in before closing it. "I had my brother park it here earlier today, he uses it when I'm out of town."

"Oh."

Emma was silent on the drive into the city from the airport, Ivan busy concentrating on the traffic didn't seem to notice, or if he did, he chose not to comment on it. She was starting to have second thoughts about this whole thing. Ivan drove a convertible, which, he had proudly informed her as they sped along the motorway, was a Ferrari four double eight spider. She knew this information should impress her, it probably impressed countless other women that he drove around in it, but Emma was not most women, and she was not impressed. What she was, was deflated. She knew that Ivan wanted to be a part of this baby's life, and Emma had thought that had meant that Ivan would, eventually, want to bring the baby to Brisbane, to spend time with his family. He couldn't very well do that in a convertible, the least child-friendly car Emma had ever seen. To be fair, he had only very recently found out that he was going to have a baby in his life, but still...He could have organised for a rental car or a taxi. Even a bus would be preferable to Emma right now, the speed at which the buildings and landscape were blurring past was starting to make her feel quite ill. By the time they pulled into Ivan's apartment complex, her legs were shaking, and she was not sure she would be able to walk in a straight line.

Ivan's apartment complex was situated right on the Brisbane river, as he busied himself with their luggage Emma heaved herself out of the car, leaning on the bonnet momentarily for support.

"Emma?" Ivan's hand snaked around her waist, "Are you all right, you look pale?"

"No," Emma tried to shake her head, but the wave of nausea that hit her put a stop to that. "Dizzy, sick." She took a deep breath. "I'll be okay, I just need to lie down." Ivan steered her towards the elevator, swiping his door key before pressing the button for the penthouse. Moments later Ivan was opening his front door for Emma, unceremoniously dropping their luggage just inside the front door, ushering Emma through to the master bedroom. Turning down the covers, he gingerly helped her to sit, bending to remove her shoes, despite her protests. Tucking her in, Ivan adjusted the air conditioning control before crossing the room to close the curtains.

"Rest as long as you need, call me if you need anything, okay?"

"I will, please don't fuss, Ivan, I just need to rest a minute, that's all."

Despite not intending to, Emma fell asleep, waking to a darkened room and no sign of Ivan. She had to admit, this room was gorgeous, and the bathroom was insanely luxurious. she was tempted to run a bath and sink into the sunken tub but thought better of it. What if Ivan was to come in and check on her? No, the bath could wait. She wandered out of the bedroom and down the hall, everywhere she looked was opulent and luxurious, and way too much of a hotel for Emma to ever be comfortable in such a place. This is where their child would stay when they spent time with Ivan she realised, her heart sinking. It would probably be what they would end up preferring, not that she would ever blame them. No, although it would no doubt hurt her heart each time they came home from Ivan's, with tales of the adventures the two would no doubt have had, it was a blessing, she knew that. Her son or daughter would have financial security, and a lot of opportunities they otherwise would not have if Ivan weren't in the picture. For that, Emma would always be grateful.

She found Ivan on the balcony, deep in conversation on the telephone, and although he gestured for her to join him, she shook her head in refusal, and instead sat on the plush sofa, flipping through one of the coffee table books piled there.

"Feeling better?"

"Yes, thank you. Sorry," she offered him a wan smile, nodding in the direction of the balcony, "I don't like heights." Ivan nodded in understanding.

"That was Marco, one of my brothers, inviting us to dinner at Xavier's house, my other brother," Ivan supplied, "you'll like them," he teased, "they are nothing like me."

"That's too bad," Emma played along, "you were starting to grow on me."

"Come on, if we leave now, I'll have time to drive nice and slow, just for you." Something about the way he spoke sent a shiver of anticipation down Emma's spine, as an image of Ivan taking her nice and slow, his head bowed at her breast, popped uninvited into her head. Unless she got a grip of her senses, this was going to be a very long night.

Ivan had been right; his brothers were nothing like him. Whereas he had an air of seriousness, his brothers were both carefree, relaxed. They greeted Emma as if they were dear old friends, and for a moment she wondered if Ivan had confided of her pregnancy to his brothers, but a subtle hand on her stomach and an arched eyebrow had Ivan shaking his head.

"Marco, are you a doctor too?" Emma asked as she helped prepare a salad to go with their dinner.

"Good grief no, I detest the sight of blood. I'm a barrister, besides," he fixed Ivan with a knowing look, "we can't all go off to war-torn countries in an effort to save the world, can we? Mother would have a fit!"

"What?" Emma gapes at Ivan, completely stunned. "You go off to war-torn countries, willingly? What if you get hurt? Or held for ransom? Or killed?" There was a traitorous catch in Emma's voice.

"He didn't tell you?" Xavier took the salad bowl from Emma and placed it on the table.

"Ivan doesn't like to talk about himself," Emma replied, her eyes never leaving Ivan's.

"Huh, interesting," Marco looks from Ivan to Emma and back to Ivan. "I wonder why that is. Could it be that you are finally considering taking dad up on his offer, brother dear?"

"Hardly." Ivan fixes his brother with a withering look. "Emma, I didn't tell you because I am not sure I will be going back. I've been considering other options, for a while now, and I didn't want you to worry unnecessarily, especially now," he glanced down at her stomach, fleetingly so, not wanting his brothers to see.

"We will talk about this later, I promise, okay? I will answer any questions you have."

"I would worry," Emma agreed.

"I know." Ivan smiled down at her, impulsively leaning closer and brushing his lips against hers. The kiss, while brief, was a question, a promise.

"Okay then."

The rest of the night passed in a state of laughter and delicious food. While Marco was happy to regale Emma with stories of their childhood exploits, Xavier showed her just why his chain of upmarket restaurants was doing so well, turning out dish after dish of exceptional food, the piece de resistance being a scrumptious sacher torte for dessert. At some point during dinner, Ivan had taken Emma's hand in his own, fingers entwined, and they had remained like that for the rest of the night. Ivan and Emma had taken their leave shortly after midnight, promising to spend the day with them tomorrow, wanting to spend as much time together as possible before heading back to Alice Springs.

"Your brothers will make the best uncles," Emma smiled across at Ivan as he drove through new deserted city streets. "Crazy, but fun." Ivan couldn't agree more.

The following day dawned bright and early, Emma felt better than she had in a long time, stopping in front of the full-length mirror on the way past, lifting up her shirt and peering at her reflection from the side, wondering if it was her imagination, or if she was really starting to grow. Ivan appeared in the mirror behind her, grinning like the proverbial cat who scored the canary.

"Just checking," Emma muttered, smoothing down her shirt.

"Don't," Ivan came around to stand before her, stilling her hands in his. "Don't be embarrassed," he slowly lifted her shirt, not breaking eye contact, "I think you are beautiful." He dropped to his knees, hands either side of her stomach, and pulled her towards him, wrapping his arms around her, his lips brushing against her stomach. "Hello, baby. Your mama and your papa can't wait to meet you, our precious miracle."

"Ivan," Emma choked out, resting her hands on his shoulders. He looked up into her face and stood slowly, arms still wrapped around her waist. Face level with hers, he brought his mouth down to claim hers, softly at first, gently. His tongue probing, seeking entrance. His arms moved higher, arching her back, his hand tangling in her hair. He deepened the kiss, his mouth hungry for more, yearning to taste all of her. Emma's breasts hardened and puckered against Ivan's chest, she could feel the length of his hardness against her thigh, she longed to have him touch her, to feel him inside her. All too soon the kiss was over, Ivan straightening Emma's hair and reluctantly stepping away from her. "Emma, thank you, for letting me be a part of this journey with you. I haven't said that yet, but I mean it. Urgh," he draws a deep breath, "if my parents were not expecting us..." he lets the sentence hang, earning a longing look from Emma, her flushed cheeks letting him know just how much she wanted him.

Ivan was in big trouble, he knew that. Every time that Emma was close to him, all he wanted to do was kiss her senseless, or whisk her off and make love to her until she screamed his name aloud. At this rate, he was never going to be able to leave the dining room table, not without a cushion in front of him in any case. Lunch at his parents' house had been a formal affair, he had not had a moment alone with Emma since they arrived. His parents had dressed up, their disapproving glances letting Ivan know how much they appreciated his low-key ensemble of jeans and a polo shirt. Despite the camaraderie of Marco and Xavier, Ivan's father had managed to mention his need for a doctor at his practice several times and was now trying to encourage Emma to take his side.

"It's a son's place, would not you agree Emma, at his father's side?"

"Certainly, when they are five or six Edward, but as a fully grown adult? No. I think it is a man's job to find his own way in the world, his own path to happiness and fulfilment."

You could have heard a pin drop, Emma instantly regretting her comment. Perhaps she should have agreed with Edward? She snuck a look at Ivan, he didn't seem angry with her, quite the opposite, he looked as if he was thinking about jumping the table and kissing her.

"You work in admin, don't you Emma?" Ivan's mother smiled at her and Emma was reminded of a viper about to strike its prey.

"Yes."

"Well, there you go then, a family practice is hardly in your wheelhouse, is it?"

"Mother," Ivan's voice held a warning.

"Well seriously darling. When you told us you were bringing someone home, we presumed it would be a potential wife, not, well," Ivan's mother gestured to Emma, "someone like her."

Emma had never seen someone's face turn as red as Ivan's did, and for a moment she was worried he might burst a valve or something.

"Really mother, someone like her? Someone kind and selfless? Someone compassionate and generous to a fault. Someone who always, always puts other people before herself? No, I guess you are right," Ivan shook his head sadly, "you would rather I marry someone shallow, someone, from money. A nice little prenup, bonus money for any children, separate bedrooms kind of marriage. Well, newsflash, I'm not interested in your kind of marriage mother. And if you are upset that I brought Emma home then this will really make your day, Emma and I-".

"Ivan, no!" Emma stood up so quickly her chair toppled backwards. "Not like this."

"You are right," Ivan nodded. "Emma and I are leaving. Marco, Xavier, I'll talk to you later." Emma scurried after Ivan, turning in the doorway.

"Thank you for lunch, it was lovely."

Emma had presumed that Ivan would take them straight back to his apartment, instead, he turned north, driving out of the city in silence, and over the lumpy bridge into Redcliffe.

"I brought you over here to show you something if you don't mind? It won't take long."

"I'd love to, I haven't been to the beach in years." Ivan wound through the leafy Redcliffe streets, keeping to the shoreline, until they reached Scarborough, turning down what was the more exclusive part of the suburb. He pulled the car up in front of an unassuming two-storey villa styled house and gestured for Emma to follow him. They passed through a side gate and into a lush garden, Emma gasped, it looked like a rainforest. The backyard sloped down to a fence, a private entrance to the shoreline awaited them. Ivan sat in the sand, Emma joining him, both of them gazing out at the horizon.

"This is my very favourite place to be Emma, to sit and think."

"Really?" Emma couldn't keep the surprise out of her voice.

"You find that surprising?"

"You don't strike me as a beachgoer. Or someone who would trespass either for that matter."

"I own this house. One day, I want to retire here, to work in private practice, one that bulk bills, to help those that really need it. I want to build my dream home here, with a cubby house and a vegetable garden." His voice was wistful, Emma could see his vision in her head, only her version had a reading nook for her to lounge in, and a little olive-skinned boy running after his papa. "I've never shown this place to anyone before Emma, but I wanted you to see, to know. My parent's life is not the one I want for my family."

"I understand, really I do. This plan of yours sounds wonderful Ivan, it really does."

Ivan knew his feelings towards Emma were changing, had already changed. It was why he had brought her here. He wanted her to share his dream, he wanted it to be their dream. Emma was different. He was not quite sure how or when or why, perhaps it had happened the first time that he had seen her, in Doctor Delaney's office, but he had fallen completely in love with her. He wanted her in his life, not just in his bed. More than that, he wanted her with him for the rest of his life, a reality that had only been made clear to him today. He watched her gaze follow that of a small family, a wistfulness to her eyes. He would not tell her, not today, not when it might cause her to run from him. No, he would wait until they were home, when this visit and his mother's nasty opinions were far behind them. He could wait. He had to. This was too important to screw up.

CHAPTER NINE

The weeks since their return from Brisbane had passed in a blur of work and comfortable conversation. Emma was now fourteen weeks along in her pregnancy, and no longer suffering any ill side effects, something for which both Emma and Ivan had been thankful for. This morning as Emma had stepped out of the shower, she had caught sight of herself in the mirror, a delighted gasp springing from her lips at the sight of a definite, yet subtle, swelling of her stomach. Finally! Proof of the life growing within, proof of her impending motherhood. Not that it would be visible to anyone who didn't know to look for it, but still, a smile curved her lips as she imagined showing Ivan when he dropped over after work tonight.

He would be on time, he always was, and she would let him in with a smile. He would gratefully accept the coffee he knew she would be offering, and as he sat at her kitchen table, slowly sipping the hot liquid, she would stand and cross to him. Standing close enough for him to touch her, she would slowly, ever so slowly, lift her shirt up until it barely skimmed the bottom of her breasts, giving him an uninterrupted view of their growing baby bump. She could picture his expression, one of amazement, could imagine the way his mouth would curl up into his trademark sexy smile. She knew he would be pleased, there was no doubt about his reaction. Emma could almost feel his gaze on her stomach, her daydream so vivid that her traitorous nipples hardened at the thought of Ivan's gaze on her body, lingering, longing, wanting. Emma gave a low moan as heat pooled between her thighs, a throbbing, aching need causing her skin to prickle and her eyes to glaze over. So lost in her visions of Ivan hearing the news, that it took Emma a while to register that her telephone was ringing.

"Hello." She snatched the receiver up from its cradle on the kitchen bench.

"Emma Roberts?" A crisp, detached voice enquired.

"Yes, speaking."

"This is Saria, I'm calling from the Alice Springs emergency department. We have you down as the next of kin for a Doctor Ivan Delgado, is that right?" Emma's heart stopped beating; her chest constricted painfully.

"Yes," she was not sure she had spoken the word aloud, was not sure she could even remember how to speak. There was a buzzing in her ears, the words that floated through were hazy, disjointed. "I'm sorry, I didn't hear you. Please, please can you repeat yourself?"

"Of course, I know this must be a bit of a shock for you, but please, you mustn't worry. As I was saying, Doctor Ivan Delgado has been involved in a traffic accident, and as his next of kin, it is our duty to inform you. If you would like to come down to the hospital, he will be remaining in the emergency department for the time being."

If? There was no if about it, she had not realised that Ivan had made her his next of kin, she suspected that was due to the baby, a way of making sure that she would always know if something happened. Emma moved about in a haze, haphazardly throwing on clothes, and gathering essential items she thought she might need. Goodness knows how long she might be staying in the emergency department. Saria was the ward clerk, unable to provide any details, and Emma didn't want to wait on the telephone while Saria fetched a doctor or nurse who might have the information Emma so desperately craved. How bad were his injuries? Was he...No, Emma refused to think of that possibility. Saria had said that Ivan would be staying in the emergency department for the time being. What did that mean? How long would he be there? Where were they thinking of moving him to? He might need surgery. Maybe they would have to fly him to Adelaide for treatment. The Royal Flying Doctor Service would transport her too, wouldn't they, as his next of kin? She really was not sure at this point.

Just in case, she flung her overnight suitcase on the bed, throwing in her laptop and mobile telephone, as well as their chargers. What if she needed to call his family? How could she reach them? Emma couldn't think straight. She had to be there, she needed to be there, at the hospital, with Ivan. Nothing else mattered right now.

Remembering the ill-fated custody agreement that Ivan had sent her in the early days of their relationship,

Emma rustled around in the kitchen drawers until she finally found it, her hand grasping it aloft in victory. She knew his lawyer's details were in there, he would know how to reach Ivan's family. Finally, after what seemed an eternity, a mere ten minutes, in reality, Emma was ready to leave the house.

She drove carefully, she knew the last thing that Ivan needed was for Emma to also be involved in a car accident, especially being pregnant. Emma was lucky enough to find a parking spot directly outside the emergency department, and she wasted no time in locking her car and sprinting up the stairs that led into the emergency department. There was a queue to see the emergency department receptionist, the frustration of not knowing combined with the stress of the situation had tears springing to Emma's eyes, she angrily brushed them away as her foot tapped out an impatient rhythm on the tiled hospital floor until it was finally her turn.

"Hi, I'm Emma Roberts, someone called to let me know Ivan Delgado was here. I'm his next of kin."

"Ivan Delgado?" The emergency department receptionist gave Emma a strange look. "I'll just check for you, I won't be a moment." Emma wondered if it was possible for anyone to type any slower, although she seriously doubted it. "Okay, here he is, he's in the acute ward, go through those doors there," the receptionist pointed around the corner, "it will be the first turn on your right."

"Thank you." Emma rushed towards the doors, fumbling to get them opened. Acute, that meant serious, Emma's stomach lurched, and she gave a final yank on the doors, they flew open and out of her grip, the deafening sound they made as they hit the emergency department reception wall reverberating throughout the entire emergency department. Seeing the sign for the acute ward, Emma hurried on.

In her desperation to get to Ivan, Emma nearly walked right by his bed, only stopping when he called out to her.

"Emma?" She spun on her heel towards his voice.

"Ivan!" She launched herself at his bed, throwing her arms around him as best she could, tears streaking down her face. "Thank heavens you are awake! I thought, I mean..." She trailed off, her eyes narrowed, her gaze wandering ever so slowly across his body, looking, mentally checking. "Why don't you look injured?" She accused, perching on the edge of the bed.

"Injured? Because I'm not, not really," Ivan finished lamely. "I have a concussion, that's all," he admitted. "What on earth are you doing here Emma? And for goodness sake, what are you wearing?"

"What do you mean what am I wearing? Clothes Ivan, they are called clothes. How badly did you hit your head?" Emma looked down at herself, seeing for the first time, in glorious clarity, just what it was that she was wearing and just why it was that she had been getting funny looks. The leopard print slippers and fluorescent pink leggings would have been fine, had they not been paired with her grandmother's vintage housecoat and a singular dangly dinosaur earring. "Oh. I see."

"Why didn't you just call me Emma?" Ivan was starting to think Emma was right, maybe he had hit his head harder than they thought? He seemed to be in an alternative universe right now.

"What?"

"On the telephone, why didn't you just call me?"

"I forgot I even had your number," Emma's face flamed. "Or a telephone." She added at the sight of his amused grin.

"Emma," Ivan started.

"Don't even," Emma commanded. "It's not funny Ivan, I thought you were mortally wounded, I thought you were dead," she hissed. "I thought...Never mind what I thought," Emma drew a shaky breath, "why didn't you tell me that you had made me your next of kin?"

"I meant to." Ivan shifted uncomfortably on the hospital bed.

"That's why I'm here since you obviously didn't see fit to call me yourself," Emma seethed. "The hospital rang me, Ivan, as your next of kin. I packed a bag and everything, I thought, you know, that we might have to go to Adelaide. I was scared."

"I'm sorry," Ivan linked his fingers through hers, squeezing them tight. "I didn't realise they would call you; I was planning on telling you myself once they released me."

"It's okay," Emma gave him a watery smile. "I know why you made me your next of kin."

"You do?" Ivan tried to breathe normally. Emma couldn't know, could she? He had been so careful.

"Yes, and I understand, I think it is very sweet, thank you." Ivan let out a breath he was not aware he had been holding, convinced now that Emma had no idea of his true intentions or reasons behind making her his next of kin. "It means a lot to me Ivan, everything that you have done for me, that you continue to do for me, to ensure that our baby will be cared for in case something happened to you," Emma spoke softly, not wishing to be overheard. "Thank you." Emma and Ivan remained like that, joined at the hands, silent, neither one knowing how much time passed, until the emergency department doctor made his rounds, coughing to make his presence known, Emma jumping off the bed in surprise, throwing Ivan a rueful look.

"Ivan," the doctor nodded at Ivan. "As I am sure you are aware, you suffered quite a nasty head wound," the doctor didn't miss the pointed look that Emma shot Ivan. "While your scans have all come back clear, we want to keep you in at least overnight for observation."

"Out of the question." Ivan's answer brooked no argument.

"Ivan, you live on grounds, don't you?" The doctor asked although Emma suspected that he already knew all of the answers.

"Yes." Ivan conceded.

"Alone?" The doctor prompted.

"Yes." Ivan bit out.

"Well, there you go. If you were the doctor making the recommendation, instead of the patient, what would you do?"

"Admit them overnight," Ivan confessed, before adding, "but there is a chance I could be wrong."

"Nice try Ivan, but you and I know the stats. Patients go home, feeling great, and relapse. You need the observation."

"So," Emma spoke without thinking, "if there was someone at home who could watch him, he could be discharged?"

"Yes, certainly," the doctor nodded. "Apart from the concussion and a few bumps and scrapes, he's fine."

"Okay then," Emma nodded, decision made.

"Emma, you don't have to," Ivan assured, earning an eye roll from Emma.

"Seriously," she muttered, "it's not a big deal Ivan. He'll stay with me," she spoke directly to the doctor. "Just let me know what it is that I have to do."

By the time Emma pulled into her driveway, she was in full nurse mode, instructing Ivan not to move until she returned from unlocking the house. She helped Ivan into the house, a task made all the more difficult because Emma insisted on slinging his arm around her shoulders in case he felt dizzy, and Ivan insisted on trying to walk by himself, the closeness to Emma having too much of an impact on his self-control. Emma soon had Ivan settled on the couch, going back for her suitcase and dumping it at the foot of her bed. She would deal with it later. Emma quickly stripped and changed her bedsheets and pillowcases, propping the pillows against the headboard, ready for Ivan. She also changed out of her crazy outfit as fast as she could, opting for the more comfortable option of track pants and a tee shirt.

"Come on," she rejoined him in the lounge room, "into bed with you."

"Emma, I'm fine really."

"I heard what the doctor said, as did you, so let's move," she picked up his hand in her own and tugged gently.

"Lead on," Ivan rose slowly, the bulge in his pants twitching as he watched Emma's rounded bottom sway from side to side as she walked. He bit down on his lip to stifle his moan of desire, longing to bite down on her, to taste her, to have her taste on his lips, in his mouth. His thoughts were doing nothing for his engorged member, throbbing with need, and it was with relief that Ivan finally made it to Emma's bedroom and slipped beneath her bedsheets. Once he was suitably comfortable, Emma cleared her throat, stepping forward to bunch Ivan's shirt in her hands.

"I need you to take this off," her eyes were looking everywhere but at him. "Please?" She asked again. Why was not he moving to help her? "Come on Ivan, off with your shirt, I need to rub this into your scrapes." She held a tube aloft for him to see.

"Emma," his voice sounded scratchy, like he had swallowed sandpaper. The thought of her, touching him, had him unable to catch his breath. Ever so slowly, he reached down and pulled his shirt up, carefully, deliberately, his eyes never leaving hers.

He saw her pupils dilate, watched her swallow hard. God how he wished that pretty little mouth of hers was wrapped around his member right now, swallowing hard, drinking him all in. He was already slick, waiting, ready, for her. Ivan couldn't ever remember having had such an intense reaction to a woman before, it was sheer torture. She sat on the bed next to him, their hips touching, and squirted some ointment onto her finger, carefully touching it to his scrapes and bruises. It was the most exquisite pain Ivan had ever experienced and he didn't bother trying to hide his deep moan. Emma's hand fluttered and stilled, she withdrew it, trembling slightly, to rest it on Ivan's chest.
"Seriously," she muttered, "doctors are such babies. Just hold still will you, I need to get this antiseptic in the right place.
"I'm fine Emma, it's okay, really. I think I'll rest now. You'll come back and check on me in an hour?" Nodding, Emma gathered up the ointment and Ivan's discarded shirt and quietly left the room.

Ivan awoke to the tempting smell of coffee, opening his eyes to discover Emma peering down at him curiously.
"What on earth are you doing?"
"I was just wondering how to go about waking you up, that's all," Emma defended, a slow blush tinting her cheeks. Ivan could think of quite a few ways but decided to keep those thoughts to himself for now. The

last thing he needed with Emma in such close proximity was to be walking around all day with an erection the size of the Eiffel tower.

"Are you this nervous around every guy you bring home Emma, or is it just me?"

"I'm not used to sharing my space, that's all, and in any case, I would not know, you are the only man who has ever been inside this house."

"You are kidding!?"

"No. There is coffee in the loungeroom, I'll meet you out there."

Emma was trying not to stare at Ivan, she really was, but she just couldn't help herself. ever since he had removed his shirt earlier, it was as if her eyes were magnets, and he was metal.

"Here," she handed him a mug of coffee as he sat on the sofa. "I want to show you something, just promise me that you are not going to freak out first, okay?"

"I shall try very hard not to." Ivan sounded dubious to Emma, but she continued regardless. Stepping around the coffee table so that she was directly in front of him, she beamed down at him, standing close enough for him to touch her.

"I have waited all day to show you this," she caught the hem of her shirt with her long fingers, pulling it up slowly, ever so slowly, until it barely skimmed the bottom of her breasts, giving him an uninterrupted view of their growing baby bump.

Ivan had never been so turned on in his entire life. Leaning forwards, he gently cupped Emma's soft bottom in his hands, drawing her closer, until she was standing between his legs. He brought his hands around to her stomach, splaying them across her rounded belly, marvelling at the life growing within, the miracle that they had created, that they were a part of. He looked up at her in awe, feathering little kisses across her stomach, seeing how he made her eyes darken. He could see the curve of her milky white breasts, longed to touch them, longed to know how they felt in his hands. Snaking a hand up and over her hip, he stroked the underside of a breast with the tip of his index finger, listening to Emma's breath hitch, watching the nipples as they peaked and hardened. She was so responsive to him, but he needed more, he wanted more. He wrapped his other arm around her waist and tugged her down onto his lap, a gasp of surprise leaving her lips as she landed atop him, his erection colliding with her core, his need obvious even through their layers of clothing.

Ivan replaced Emma's hands with his own, removing her shirt fully, revealing a soft pink coloured lace bra. Ivan traced the swell of her breast through the lace, before unclipping her bra and discarding it to one side. With her breasts now free, Ivan weighed them in his hands.

"Perfect," he murmured, "just perfect." Lowering his mouth, Ivan captured a nipple between his teeth, biting gently. Spasms of pleasure shot through Emma and she arched her back, moaning as heat pooled between her thighs, a throbbing, aching need causing her skin to prickle and her eyes to glaze over. Ivan's tongue darts over Emma's nipple, licking, sucking. It was better than all of his fantasies.

"Ivan?" Tentative, unsure of herself. He lifts his head, the foggy haze of desire subsiding slowly as reality returns.

"Emma, I-" Shame fills him. He had rushed her, after he had sworn to wait.

"Shh," she places a finger over his lips, smiling. "We have to stop, you have a concussion, I want you to want me because you want me, not because your brain is addled, and I don't want this to be something you regret tomorrow."

Ivan knew Emma was right, not that it made it any easier to stand up and walk away from her. A cold shower was what he needed. A cold shower and a stern talking to.

Naked from the waist up, her nipples were still hard. Emma had no idea they could ache so, she longed to have them once again inside Ivan's mouth, his tongue deliciously circling her pebbled nipple. Instead, she yanked her shirt back on, forgoing the bra, and went to fetch the mop. Cleaning, that is what she would do. Scrubbing the house always gave her time to think.

Cleaning certainly gave Emma time to think, and horrified by her reaction to Ivan, to his every touch and every look, she vows to stay away from him as much as possible while he is here. Only another day, she repeats again and again to herself, only another day.

Later, as she stands under the water in the shower, washing away all evidence of Ivan's touch, she reasons that it must be due to all the hormones currently flooding her body, and the fact that he is under the safe roof as she is, that is all. There is absolutely no other reason for it, she consoles herself. None at all. As her heart continues to ache, she is forced to admit what she has already known. She is in love with Ivan. Somehow, when she was not looking, he snuck into her heart. And for Emma, that was a very big problem. She knew that Ivan lusted after her, she also knew that once she hit her third trimester, that lust would likely fade. She had met his parents, she was not stupid. She knew that there was no way someone like Ivan would ever fall in love with someone like her, she knew that the only future they had together was as friends, for the sake of their child. She had not even been looking for a relationship. So why then did she feel so lost, so bereft, when he was not around?

CHAPTER TEN

The last three days had been sheer torture for Ivan. He had remained at Emma's house for a second day, both of them very careful to avoid touching each other, even accidentally. When Emma stepped backwards from removing their dinner from the oven on the last night, colliding with Ivan who had been gaping at her rounded bottom unseen, she lurched a mile in the air, dropping the pan and scalding her hand in the process. Seething, she had allowed Ivan to dress it for her, before shooing him from the kitchen to clean up by herself, replacing their roast with a stack of sandwiches instead. He was finally back in his own accommodation, which should have made him relieved, but only served to make him restless. He wanted to be with Emma. In every sense of the word. He knew she wanted him, or at the very least, that she lusted after him to some degree, her own body confirmed her attraction every time he touched her. Ivan couldn't ever recall being with a woman who was as responsive to his touch as Emma was. It was a heady aphrodisiac.

He knew he needed to be careful with Emma, there was something about her, a vulnerability that she kept hidden just below the surface. He had spooked her with his reaction to her the other day, he knew that. She had wanted to share her growing stomach with him, and he had been too turned on to think straight. The sight of her, standing before him, showing him physical proof that his child was nestled there, growing within her, had been his downfall. She was stunning. He had meant simply to kiss her stomach, to croon words of love to his unborn child, but once he touched her, he craved more. He needed to feel her bottom between his hands, had to know if it was as soft and delectable as it looked. Her softs mews encouraged him further, and he was only too happy to accept, moving upwards. He had longed to feel her breasts in his hands for weeks, had lain awake at night wondering if they would pucker under his touch, imagining the taste of them on his tongue. The reality had been far greater than anything he could have thought up, the frustration that followed an intense battle of wills. He had overstepped the invisible line he had drawn.

Ivan knew his frustration was making him short-tempered at work, usually unflappable, he had snapped at his junior doctors today and was currently being avoided by his interns. He knew, he had seen them do a quick about-face and scurry in the opposite direction from him, all huddled in a group, moving as one. Worse still, was the way he had snapped at Emma. Storming down to the switchboard to have his entire team paged at once had seemed like a good idea when he failed to reach any of them on their mobile telephones, what followed was entirely his own fault. He chose Emma's window, just being near her was enough to calm him, happy to wait while her manager spoke with her, unable to avoid overhearing their conversation, ears perking up at Emma's agreement to cover a sixteen-hour shift without notice. Finished, she turned, her smile dying on her lips as she catches sight of Ivan's expression. Punching some numbers into her keyboard, she points to the telephone on the wall next to the window, Ivan snatching it up on the first ring.

"Ivan, what's wrong?"

"You are working a sixteen-hour shift tonight?"

"We're short-staffed," she confirmed, nodding absently.

"In your condition?" Ivan raised his eyebrow at her.

"Ivan-" Emma's voice held a warning, one which was cut off mid-sentence by Ivan.

"Forget it, page my team for me switchboard, I want them here, now," he knew calling her by her title would annoy her. His barb hit, he heard Emma's soft gasp of surprise, saw an angry tint flush her cheeks, her shoulders stiffen. "All of them."

"Of course, doctor." Emma's fingers raced across the keyboard. "Done." She dismissed him without a glance, answering another call before he had even left the window. He crossed to the other side of the corridor, waiting for his staff members to arrive, intending to brief them on a new case that was referred to them, instead, once they had all gathered around him, he found himself giving them a dressing down instead, one young intern fleeing the group in tears.

"We are trauma surgeons; we don't have the luxury of waiting until after lunch or when it is convenient for us. If you ever keep me waiting for twenty minutes again, without a single word, you are out of my team, is that understood? There is no excuse. You all have telephones; you should all know what the switchboard number is by now. This is a small hospital, if you can't be in front of me in under two minutes, you advise switchboard, end of discussion." As Ivan moved his team away from the switchboard, Emma noticed he looked tired, too tired maybe? He was right, it was a small hospital, maybe he was working too hard? Emma knew that he would only deny it if she confronted him with it, stubborn as he was. He needed an early night, despite being put out with her working hours, Emma knew that he worked far more than he let on. If no one else called in sick to work, she should be able to manage to get away on time. She would go home and change, and then pop back here and cook dinner for Ivan. Her plan set; Emma settled back into the routine of her day.

Home, at last, Ivan tossed his jacket across the arm of the sofa, and grabbed a bottle of beer out of the fridge, opening up the sliding door that led to his handkerchief-sized patio. He was glad to see the end of today. A shrill ring jolted him out of his reverie, a curse leaving his lips.

"Hello," he barked out, expecting it to be the hospital calling him.

"Ivan, it's Emma."

"Emma," guilt flooded him, "how can I help you?"

"You can stop acting as if you don't know me, and come and open the back gate, my arms are full."

"What back gate? Wait, here?" Ivan wandered out the front door and across the basketball court to the back staff gate. "Okay, I see you," he disconnected the call. Letting her in, he took the bags and quietly led her back across the basketball court to his apartment.

"Emma, what on earth are you doing here? Someone could have seen you." Ivan shut the front door firmly behind him, turning to really look at Emma. Something was different about her tonight. She was wearing a soft floral summer dress that fitted her curves like a glove, a row of tiny buttons on the bodice. She seemed nervous.

"Worried about your reputation Ivan?"

"No, yours." Emma smiled.

"Well, don't worry. If people want to talk, let them. Tonight is about what you need."

"What?" Ivan's heart skipped a beat, hardly daring to hope.

"I was thinking about you this afternoon," she whispered softly. "About why you were so cranky earlier. You look tired." Emma advanced slowly towards Ivan, smiling. "I had planned to come and make you dinner, and then I thought," she stood toe to toe with Ivan, her chest touching his, "dessert would be better." Ever so slowly Emma popped her top button undone, then the next, and finally the third, while Ivan watched, mesmerized.

"Emma." Ivan stilled her hands in his. "If you stay…" he moved away from her, his sentence hung in the air between them. What she wrong to agree to come here?

She swallowed thickly as her eyes followed him around the room, his movements agitated.

"No strings attached, Ivan," Emma began, "I promise I won't expect you to marry me or make promises that you can't keep."

"Emma," Ivan stilled, his voice was molten honey, sending delicious shivers of desire down her spine, "you don't have to do this."

"I want to. I want you."

"I want you too." Ivan stalked towards Emma, slowly, deliberately. Reaching her, he cupped her face gently in both of his hands, rubbing the pad of his thumb across her tempting lips, before bringing his mouth down to hers, his tongue softly parting her lips, entering her mouth with confidence.

He angled her face, deepening the kiss, his tongue delving deeper inside, tasting every inch he could. His hands tangled in her hair, holding her, guiding her. Ivan's fingers moved to Emma's dainty buttons, undoing them easily, slipping a hand inside to knead her breast through her bra, grinning when he felt the instant tightening of her nipples. Drawing back, he tugged her dress up and over her head, tossing it aside, quickly pulling off his shirt and adding it to the pile. Who would ever have thought that rosebud pink lace could be so enticing? Ivan reached around to unclip Emma's bra, chuckling when she crossed her arms over her chest, suddenly shy.

"Don't ever think you need to hide Emma, you are stunning." Ivan gently moved her hands away from herself, cupping a breast in his hand, while his other hand snaked around her waist to draw her closer. He bent his head to capture her breast, teasing her nipple until he felt it harden and pebble beneath his tongue, suckling and biting, loving the sounds it elicited from Emma. He could smell her arousal mixed with his, the air around them was thick with longing and need.

His hands roamed down her back, hooking his thumbs into the waistband of her panties, he started to tug them down, slowly, gradually becoming aware of the fact that Emma had stopped making any sound at all. She stood perfectly still. Ivan stilled; something was wrong.

"Emma?" She would not meet his gaze.

"I'm sorry, I can't," she rasped. "I don't know what, I mean, I don't know how, I've never, um," her face flamed red, she hung her head, covering her face with her hands. Was Emma saying what Ivan thought she was saying?

"Emma? Are you a virgin?"

"Yes." She shrugged. "I'm sorry, I should have told you earlier, I just...I wanted you, like that, desperately. I thought you would say no if you knew. I'm sorry," she chewed her lip.

Ivan crushed her to him, a fierce craving, a possessive longing blazing within. Emma was a virgin, and she wanted him, she wanted her first time to be with him. His heart was singing, surely this meant that she cared for him, even on some level? Scooping her up into his arms, Ivan carried her through to his bedroom, stopping at the foot of the bed.

"Emma, are you sure?" Ivan tore himself away from her mouth to ask, barely breathing, hoping. He had to know this was what she wanted too, not just because she was caught up in the moment, he had to hear her say it. Emma pulled his mouth back down to hers.

"I'm sure," she stated, knowing that he needed to hear her say it. "I want you, Ivan, no one else." Emma didn't care that it was only for one night. She was pregnant, admittedly through a clinical error, but still, she was pregnant with Ivan's baby, his son or daughter, growing safely within. She had lost her heart to him, so for tonight, she would also lose her body. She would be his, completely, no matter what the consequences were.

Ivan finished undressing Emma with reverence, kneeling before her to feather kisses across her slightly rounded stomach, gathering her close to him, marvelling that his child, their child, was nestled in there, contentedly growing. Emma reached down and tugged at his shirt, and he laughingly moved his arms from around her waist, standing up and stripping his clothes off, standing naked before her, his hard member jutting out proudly. He stood, transfixed, as Emma's eyes roamed across his chest and down, her tongue flicking across her lips at the sight of his erection. Gathering her close to him, Ivan laid her back on his bed, loving the fact that she didn't try to hide her body from his gaze. Ivan's gaze raked over her body, drinking her in, committing her to memory. Slowly, very slowly, he leant down, capturing Emma's mouth in a kiss that left nothing to the imagination. Ivan's hand slid down, gliding over Emma's stomach and down further, to cup her centre, earning a surprised gasp from Emma. Ivan grew harder still at the discovery of her wetness, his cock twitching at the knowledge that he was the one who had made her that wet.

Ivan ran his index finger along Emma's seam, slowly, before carefully pushing it past her silky folds, and into Emma's tight core, probing, testing. Having found no physical barrier, Ivan sighed contentedly, not wanting to do anything that would cause Emma pain. He dipped his finger in and out of Emma's dripping core with a leisurely speed, relishing the feel of Emma moaning and writhing beneath him. Breaking their kiss, Ivan smiled down at Emma, her lips swollen, face all flushed. Resting on his haunches, he drew Emma's legs up and over his shoulders, never breaking eye contact, wanting, needing to make sure she was comfortable. He watched her as his tongue darted out and probed into her very core, teasing, tasting, drinking in her juices, her hips jerked and bucked beneath him, her breathing growing laboured with each flick of his tongue. Knowing she was close, Ivan rose to his knees, spreading her legs even further apart, wanting to see all of her, loving the sight of having her open for him, knowing that she was his alone.

"You are so beautiful," he breathed, before settling himself between her legs. Plucking a condom from the bedside table, he opened it and rolled it on. Using his hand to guide his erection, he pushed into her tight, wet, core, slowly, so as not to cause any discomfort.

Once Ivan was fully buried inside Emma, he stilled, giving her a moment to adjust to him, to his size and weight, to the feel of him, before pulling out fully and driving in again. Ivan had planned to go slowly, carefully, for Emma's first time, instead, he found that Emma arched her back and bucked her hips to meet his powerful thrusts, screaming in pleasure as he drove in harder and deeper, his thick member filling her to breaking point, his pelvic bone pressing against her sensitive nub. Emma was on fire, she couldn't tell where she ended and Ivan began. Emma held nothing back as Ivan moved within her, she was his completely.

"Come for me Emma," Ivan urged, knowing she was close. Pulling his length out fully, he gave one final thrust all the way into her core and felt her walls tighten around his stiffened member as he pushed her over the edge, hearing her scream out his name with wild abandon. With one final thrust he exploded inside her, gripping her hips for support, until totally spent, he collapsed beside her.

Never in his life had Ivan experienced such a powerful orgasm, and never a simultaneous one. He slid out of Emma slowly, discarding the condom, holding her close, not wanting to be apart from her even for one second. He looked down at Emma, her face flushed from her orgasm, a slow smile spreading across her face. Her nipple was still hard, he couldn't resist flicking his finger over it, surprised to feel himself harden again so soon. Ivan could scarcely believe it, Emma had just given him the most mind-blowing orgasm of his life, more than that, she had given herself to him fully, without reservation. The thought of Emma being with anyone else after tonight had Ivan growling within. She was his. He had claimed her, the thought of someone else touching her, of another man making her cum, of her sweet lips screaming another man's name, was abhorrent to Ivan. No, he had to marry her, he had to convince her to take a chance on him, had to prove to her that he would not let her down, that he loved her, for her, not just for the baby.

Emma trailed her hand over Ivan's chest, loving the feel of it beneath her skin. She wondered if she dare? Her fingers danced lower still; she could sense Ivan watching her.

"Emma!" Ivan gasped, as her hands closed around his thick shaft, slowly starting to slide her hand up and down.

"What?" She asked, uncertain, her hands stalling. "You don't like it?"

"God, no! It feels amazing Emma," Ivan reassured, gathering her close. "I just don't want you to think that you need to do this for me, ever. Or anything else that might make you uneasy. Tonight is about you, I want to give you pleasure, I want you to know what that is like, with me."

"I want to touch you too." Emma scooted to the other end of the bed. "I want you to feel pleasure," a blush darkened her features, "and I want to be the one to give that to you." Emma trailed her fingers up his inner thighs, leaning over him carefully, taking a delicate testicle into her mouth, sucking gently, rolling it around her mouth like she would a rum ball, savouring the texture, the taste, the sounds he made because of her.

Emma shifted her focus to Ivan's aching shaft, her tongue darting around the rim and over the top, before slowly lowering her mouth down over his hardened length. Ivan watched as Emma explored his length, working out what he enjoyed best. Ivan decided that he had never seen anything so hot as watching his length slide in and out of Emma's mouth, certain he would explode. Emma shifted her weight on the bed, taking him all the way into her hot mouth. She gripped his hips, her hair tickling his inner thighs as she bobbed up and down.

"Emma!" Ivan's cry was frantic. "I...can't...hold...on...Urgh!" Emma increased her speed, sensing what he needed. "Emma...yes, yes, yes...Emma...I...oh...Emma!" Ivan came with a shout, her name a prayer on his lips, his orgasm ripping through him, his hips bucking wildly beneath Emma, who held on, continuing to suck him until he had no more seed to empty into her. Pulling Emma into his arms, his mouth meeting hers, Ivan could taste himself in her mouth, his insatiable member growing hard again at the thought. Would he ever tire of her?

He reached out and traced her nipple, causing it to pucker at his touch. Rising to his knees, he bent his head to enclose her puckered nipple, earning a deeply satisfied moan from Emma. He flicked his tongue over it, suckling it before nipping it between his teeth, causing Emma to cry out and arch her back, thrusting her breasts towards him. Ivan drew Emma up to her knees, turning her around and guiding her head down onto the bed. He ran his hands down her back and across her bottom, using the back of her thighs to push her knees further apart. With her legs parted and her bottom in the air, Ivan could see Emma's slick folds, already coated in her juices. As he rolled on a condom, he bent his head, he needed to taste her. Just a little taste, he reasoned, as his tongue lapped at her sensitive nub. Emma's soft mews encouraged him further, his tongue pushed into her core, tasting her as he inhaled her musky scent. He drank in her juices, savouring the taste. With a moan he gripped his throbbing length, placing it at the entrance to her core.

With his hands on her hips, he plunged into her from behind, a grunt of satisfaction leaving his body as her walls stretched to accommodate his engorged member with a delighted gasp from Emma. Oh, she was so tight, so tight and perfect. Just for him. His, that's what she was, his and his alone. For tonight, for always. It was a heady thought, sharing this with Emma, every single day, and nearly Ivan's undoing. He stilled, slowing down. No, he reminded himself, Emma first, Emma would always come first, in every way. Ivan snaked his arm around Emma's waist, sliding down further, using his fingers to touch and tease her bundle of nerves as he moved inside her. Emma urged him on, grunting and pleading, as he moved in and out of her from behind, with exquisite slowness. Ivan revelled in Emma's wetness, relishing the very feel of her, the way his balls felt against her bottom as he rocked back and forth into her with firm, deep strokes until he felt her climax building again. Ivan moved faster, frantic with need, so close to his release, fuelled by Emma's cries for him to go faster, harder, deeper. Exploding together, Emma's walls gripped Ivan's shaft tightly as he emptied his need deep inside of her, filling her, until they both collapsed on top of the bed, limbs entwined, totally spent.

Emma had made a very big mistake; she saw that now. She had told Ivan that this would be a one-night kind of deal, just to scratch an itch, to lose her virginity, to know what it felt like, just once. She was wrong, she knew that now. No matter how long she lived, she would never be able to forget the way Ivan was with her, the way he moved inside of her, the way he seemed to fit, perfectly, as if they were two halves, as if they belonged. Although Emma had nothing to compare Ivan to, she already knew that it would be futile, she would never be able to replicate what she had with him with anyone else. She didn't want to. Which was the problem. In a few short hours, she would leave to go home to her own little house. Ivan would leave to go to work. Their night would be over. She knew she would keep her word; she would not ask for a repeat night. She would not become that possessive, jealous ex-lover. Instead, she would revert back to being friends with Ivan, she had to, for their child. Tonight was it, all she got of Ivan Delgado. It would be enough, it had to be. It would be her one thing to get her through the rest of her life.

Ivan had never been more spent in his life, or more turned on. Being with Emma was a heady experience that he was fast becoming addicted to, with her, everything just felt right, even the way her luscious breasts currently felt against his chiselled chest was exactly as it should be. He wished that he could just tell her, admit to her the truth, let her know that he had fallen in love with her. If she only knew, then maybe he could ask her for more time, time he could use to show her how compatible they were, not just in the bedroom. Time he could use to stall, to woo her, properly, so that she might come to care for him, to love him even. But he didn't have time. There was a baby already making his or her presence known in their lives, no matter how he felt towards Emma, their baby would come first, always. Ivan wanted to know everything about Emma, every quirk, every detail. In years to come, these are the little things that he would remember, he was certain of it.

"Where are your parents? Your family?" The question caught Emma off guard. Laying naked in Ivan's arms, she felt exposed, vulnerable.

"They live in town, as does my sister and her husband."

"You are kidding?!" Now it was Ivan's turn to be surprised. "Why haven't I met them? You never talk about them, I just assumed that they weren't nearby."

"We aren't close." Emma sighed, then turned to face Ivan. "You can meet them if you would like to, they would love you." She hated how bitter she sounded.

"You don't want me to meet them?" Ivan brushed away the tear that spilled from Emma's eye and down her face.

"No." It was a hoarse whisper.

"Why not? Do you think they would object to me being in the baby's life?"

"They don't know about the baby."

"Emma! You are almost five months pregnant, in a couple more weeks you'll be showing, you won't be able to hide it anymore. You need to tell them."

"I don't want to Ivan, you don't understand. Your parents might be a bit...Entitled, but they love you, it is obvious in every word they speak, even if perhaps they didn't show it in actions as much as they should have done. My parents aren't like that. They have never made it a secret that they prefer my younger sister over me, it has always been known."

"Are you serious?" Ivan didn't know what to say. His parents had been, at times, distant emotionally, and they had not always been there physically, but he and his brothers had always known that they were loved. They were treated fairly and had all the same opportunities to pursue their dreams. He couldn't imagine growing up knowing that you were unwanted, that your sibling was preferred over you.

"Yes. Amazingly enough, it didn't ruin my relationship with my sister. I'm not bitter that she had every opportunity in life, she deserves it, she is incredibly unselfish, but it did ruin the relationship that I have with my parents. Every single thing that I ever did was always compared to her, unfavourably." Emma shrugged.

"When I took the job at the hospital, they were upset that I didn't have a career like my sister. Despite paying my sister's tuition, they lectured me about the fact that I should have gone to university, that I could have worked my way through like other kids had." Emma rolled her eyes. "My house will never be nice enough or big enough, I will never be pretty enough or smart enough, nothing I do or say or am will ever be enough for them." Emma ran her palm down the side of Ivan's face. "You, Ivan, would be enough. You would be perfection. If I took you to meet my parents, they would adore you. You are a doctor," Emma drew an imaginary tick in the air, "rich," another tick, "handsome," another tick. "If they meet you and then you disappear, because you will, we both know that you are not going to remain in Alice Springs until this baby is eighteen," she rests her hand across her abdomen, "it will be me that has to deal with the fallout, not you."

"Emma," Ivan pulled her closer, "that is not going to happen, you know that, right?"

"I know that you will always be here, maybe not physically, for our baby, I believe that, but we are not an item, we never were, and that isn't going to change. If I announce my pregnancy, take you home to meet everyone, and then not marry you, it will be the last straw for them."

"I'm sorry." It seemed inadequate somehow to Ivan, apologizing, he wished he could do more.

"Don't ever apologize for this Ivan, it was my choice, my decision. I'm sorry you were dragged into it, this was not exactly your life plan, was it?"

"No," I replied truthfully. "You remember I told you about my cancer scare, while we were in Brisbane? How that was the reason that the clinic had my sample in the first place?" Ivan looked at Emma, who nodded her head. She remembered, it was seared on her brain, that memory. She had cried about it later, once she knew that she loved him, she had cried for how scared he must have been, for how fragile life was, for the fact that they had been thrown together at all, how their fate could have been so much different. "Well," Ivan continued, "it was done more as an afterthought, not as a life plan. Don't get me wrong, I would not give this up for the world," he stroked her stomach, "but no, it was not something that I had hoped and wished for. Not the same way you have Emma. Will you think about letting them know, about letting me meet them? That is all I ask. I worry about you, I don't want you to ever be alone in this parenting gig, for any reason."

"I promise I'll think about it." Emma conceded.

"Good." Ivan smiled down at her, a predatory gleam in his eyes. He captured one of her sweet pink nipples in his mouth, sliding his arm beneath her to cup her bottom. He tugged her closer until her sex was flush against his erected shaft. It stunned him, his attraction to her, his primal need to have her, the way a single look from her had him coming undone. His other hand parted her silky folds, plunging a finger deep into her core, Emma rewarding him with an excited moan and an unexpected buck of her hips. He slid his finger in and out of her, enjoying the feeling of her becoming wetter and wetter under his ministrations until his need for her became more pressing, and he pulled back, both of them gasping. As Ivan went to shift his weight, Emma stopped him with her outstretched hand.

"No." She rose to her knees, straddling him. "I want to see what you see."

"Hotter than hell," Ivan muttered, soaking in the view of Emma's heavy breasts, the swell of her stomach, even her bundle of nerves at the apex of her thighs. "I've never been more turned on," he confessed, "than I am with you telling me what you want, you sexy, liberated minx."

Emma giggled delightedly at the compliment. She could feel the thick head of Ivan's erection nudging against her sensitive nub. Smiling lazily, she leant over his chiselled chest to kiss him deeply, her nipples grazing against his firm chest. His hands glided down her sides, cupping her bottom and pressing her firmly against his erection. Emma moved her hips in small circles as she deepened the kiss, her nub rubbing against Ivan's hard length, teasing him slowly, gasping and jerking away from his mouth when his hand slipped in between them and gave her nub a hard tweak, shooting spasms of pleasure to her very core. Straightening up, with Ivan's hand still kneading and rolling her nub between his fingers, Emma plucked a condom from the dresser and unwrapped it, rolling it down Ivan's shaft, then, with a wink, she grasped Ivan's erection, using her hand to guide his throbbing length deep inside of her aching centre. Ivan watched in fascination as Emma slowly slid down the length of his shaft, almost all the way, and then slid back up again, torturously slowly, with a wicked smile on her gorgeous face.

Desperate with need and unable to stand the wait any longer, Ivan released her nub, before reaching up and grabbing hold of her hips, pulling her all the way down on his shaft in one swift move, drawing a surprised gasp from Emma's parted lips. Ivan nearly came undone as he watched his shaft disappear completely into Emma's centre, feeling her muscles stretch to accommodate his size. She was mesmerising, he decided as he watched her arch her back, flinging her head back as she sang his name, taking him deeper still. He started to move inside her, his eyes feasting on the sight of her, hypnotised by the way her breasts swayed and danced for him as she met and rode every one of his thrusts, the way she threw her head back in a scream of triumph as she orgasmed atop of him, bucking her hips as her release tore through her. Gripping his hips, Emma called his name, tipping him over the edge and grinding down onto him until his spasms stopped, collapsing onto his chest with a contented sigh.

They spent the rest of the right like that, curled up in each other's arms, committing each other to memory, not wanting to lose even one second of time together. As the shadows on the walls started to appear, she smiled up at Ivan from between her lashes, the memory of last night lingering in the air between them. She ached in places she didn't even know existed. Ivan's gaze raked over her body, a slow flush tinted her cheeks and she self-consciously reached for the sheet, discarded sometime during the night. A deep laugh rumbled up from Ivan.

"Leave it, you are exquisite," he instructed, drawing Emma closer and claiming her mouth with a kiss that left her in no doubt as to his desire for her. He slid a hand down to her centre, growing hard when he discovered that she was already wet for him. Shifting position, he pushed her knees up, letting them fall to her sides. She was completely open for him, splayed out, leaving nothing hidden. He grinned wickedly up at her before teasing her sensitive nub with his tongue, claiming it with his mouth and sucking gently, as she writhed beneath him. He moved down to her silky folds, sliding his tongue inside, teasing, tasting her juices. Pulling her knees over his shoulders, he continued to slide his tongue in and out, flicking her nub with his fingers, pinching, rolling it between his thumb and forefinger as she bucked her hips beneath him, her breathing growing shallow.

"Ivan!" she pleaded, clutching at his hips, "please!"

"Please what? Tell me what you need honey." His breath sent a cool breeze over her core, increasing her sensitivity. He wanted to hear her say it, he needed to hear it.

"I want you. Inside me. Now!" she panted. Ivan smiled, reaching over to the bedside table he extracted a condom and unwrapped it, slipping it on.

With Emma's legs still dangling over his shoulders, he rose to his knees, leaning over her and using her legs as support, he drove his hardened length into her, before pulling out fully and driving in again and again. Emma arched her back and bucked her hips to meet his powerful thrusts, screaming in pleasure as he drove in harder and deeper, his thick member hitting her G spot.

"Ivan, oh my god, Ivan, yes, yes!" Emma held nothing back as he moved within her, caressing his ego with her mews and moans, urging him deeper with her words.

"Come for me Emma," Ivan ordered, knowing she was close. Pulling his length out fully, he gave one final thrust all the way into her core and felt her walls tighten around his stiffened member as he pushed her over the edge, hearing her scream out his name with wild abandon. With one final thrust he exploded inside her, gripping her hips for support, until totally spent, he collapsed beside her.

It was Emma who broke the spell, sitting up slowly, looking at Ivan with a mixture of sadness and ruefulness.

"I need to go; it will be daylight soon."

"Sneaking out before dawn?" Ivan tried to lighten the mood, but it only served to depress him. "Emma, you don't have to go, you know. Why don't you stay?"

There, he had said it. He had addressed the elephant in the room.

"You have work Ivan, you need space to get into the zone," she started hunting around the room for her clothes, dressing slowly. "Besides, we both know that the last thing either of us want is to be a part of some trashy hospital gossip. I have today off, so I will probably just sleep anyway, but I am back at work tomorrow, so you will still see me, Ivan, this isn't goodbye." So why the hell did it feel like it was?

CHAPTER ELEVEN

Emma felt strangely alone. Ivan had gathered her to him in the doorway of his bedroom, had said goodbye before lowering his mouth to kiss her thoroughly, slowly, gently, at first, his hands tangling in her hair. He had not wanted to let her go; she knew he had to. She could feel the weight of his erection against her thigh, had marvelled at the way his appetite for her was insatiable, as hers was for him. She had been tempted, oh so tempted, to simply reach out and stroke him, to feel his length once more in her hands, to press her hands into the muscles on his back, as he bore down into her. She knew he wanted her, as much as she wanted him, there was no doubt. Her aching core reminded her of just how much Ivan wanted her. It was a delicious sort of ache, one that can only come from hours of being stabbed into by a lover's hardened length. Emma had been apprehensive at first, Ivan's member was thicker and longer than she had ever imagined, and she had spent quite a bit of time imagining it, but she had nothing to worry about. Ivan had been everything that she knew he would be in a lover, generous and sensitive, and she had easily stretched to accommodate him.

Emma's house was quiet, too quiet. She already missed Ivan. Peeling off her clothes she threw them in the wash, before turning her shower onto the hottest she could stand and stepping in. Relaxed from her shower, Emma stretched out on her bed, intending to have a short nap being tackling her chores, but she just couldn't get comfortable. There was an ache inside her, a tight coil of need and desire, just begging to be released. Her hand trailed lazily across her breast, she tweaked her nipple, hard, just as Ivan had. A spasm shot through her. She rolled her nipple between her thumb and finger, increasing the pressure slowly, pinching and pulling the engorged nipple, writhing around, wetness pooling between her legs. Her other hand moved further down, quickly finding her sensitive nub among her hair. She fingered her nub, twisting it in circles, pulling, tweaking, twisting it. Emma could feel the pressure rising as she fingered her nub even faster. The combination of her pinching and pulling at her engorged nipple while fingering her nub was potent. In her mind she was seeing Ivan, feeling Ivan, touching her, entering her. With a triumphant shout, she tipped over the edge, still pinching, and pulling at her engorged nipple while fingering her nub, slowly now, as the waves of orgasm started to fade away.

After her release yesterday, Emma had spent most of the day running errands and thinking about Ivan. It was not until she went to get out of her car and discovered that she had dampened through her panties with thoughts of Ivan, that she decided that she would try not to think about Ivan for the rest of that day, that thoughts of Ivan were best kept for when she was alone in her own house and had the time and space to play uninterrupted. Honestly, she had never been more exhausted! She was glad to be getting back to work, at least she would get a break from her invasive thoughts. She had also been thinking about what Ivan had said to her, not just what he had done to her and for her, and Emma was starting to think that maybe she would call her parents this weekend after all, maybe Ivan had been right, maybe they did deserve to know that she was pregnant. Who knows, her ever hopeful inner voice piped up, maybe they would even be happy, for her, with her. Maybe they would be glad to embrace grandparenthood.

Emma had set her alarm earlier than usual today, kneeling on the floor in front of her full-length mirror, wanting to know just how she looked when her own fingers played with her nub. It was heady, seeing her fingers roll her nub around, pinching it hard, pulling it as far as it would stretch. Her juices coated her opening, all slick and sticky, and she tentatively pushed one finger inside. Seeing her reflection in the mirror was more of a turn-on than Emma imagined, and it was not long before the foggy haze of her release clouded her vision. Feeling freer than she had ever felt before, Emma took her time in showering and getting ready for work. There was, she decided, quite literally nothing that could ruin her day. A point that was proven to her when she went to get into her car, discovering a single red rose placed carefully on the bonnet, a ribbon attached to an envelope. Opening it, a key fell into her hand, with a note that simply read: My place, after work today, let yourself in. Ivan x. She knew she shouldn't go, that she should walk away now before her heart became even more damaged, but she also knew that she would not. She knew that she would go and be with him, no matter the consequences.

Emma loved working the weekends, it meant that she had the switchboard office to herself, that she didn't have to make polite conversation or pretend to care about the topics everyone else was discussing. The day moved at a steady pace, Emma chatting with several of the new doctors who arrived to collect their accommodation packs, all eager to be starting their new positions. Emma loved this part of her job, talking to people, learning their stories. The new staff were always keen to introduce themselves to switchboard staff, keen to get on their good side and to make a good first impression. As Emma stood chatting and laughing at something one of the new arrivals was saying, she glanced up to see Ivan standing nearby, watching her. She grew warm under his gaze, loving the way his smile bloomed on his face and the way his mouth formed the word later. She nodded imperceptibly, yes; she would be there.

Just before lunch, there was a slight tap on Emma's switchboard window. Emma indicated that she was on the telephone, but that she would not be long. Ending her call, she turned to the lady at the window.

"Hi, how can I help you?" Emma asked. The woman was stunning, Emma was not sure she had ever actually seen anyone quite as stunning as this lady. Emma had seen pretty people, and beautiful people, but the woman blew them all out of the water, she was mesmerising. Crystal clear blue eyes with a waterfall of blonde locks cascading down her back, Emma wondered if she might have been a model.

"Hi, my name is Lori Masters, I'm going to be working here for the next couple of weeks, I was told that there would be an accommodation pack for me to collect from the switchboard, I was hoping you could point me in the right direction please?"

"Of course, Lori, this," Emma gestured with her arms open wide, "is the switchboard."

"Oh, wonderful! I am not too good with directions," Lori confessed with a grin.

"Oh, I know what you mean," Emma agreed, "I know how to get to a place, but I couldn't tell you the address of that place. One of my many weird quirks." Emma smiled, sensing a great working relationship with this new doctor.

"Let me see if we have your accommodation pack yet, sometimes there can be a slight delay in bringing them over." Emma crossed to the bench where all of the accommodation packs were stacked and waiting for collection, flicking through until she found the M's. "Okay, here it is, Masters." Emma held it up, looking for any extra notes that might have been included. Oh no, they had given her the wrong key. They had written down Ivan's unit number instead of Lori's.

"Lori I am really sorry, but it looks as if they have given you the wrong key, they have given you a key for a unit where one of our doctors are already staying."

"Oh, no, that's okay," Lori was quick to reassure.

"I'll see if I can find anyone over at the accommodation office who might be able to fix it for you." Emma picked up the telephone, but Lori interrupted.

"Oh no. I meant, it is okay, I am supposed to be staying with someone."

"Oh, okay. We don't get a lot of doctors happy share accommodation, I guess they must have been really short of rooms." Emma shrugged.

"I guess it does help that he is my fiancé." Lori blushed at her confession.

"I'm sorry, what?" Emma was not sure she had heard Lori correctly.

"I said I guess it does help that he is my fiancé."

"You are going to be staying with your fiancé?" Emma clarified.

"Yes," Lori was starting to look worried. "I mean...That's okay, isn't it, it won't get him into trouble, or anything will it?"

"No," Emma could barely speak. "He won't get into trouble." At least not in the way that Lori was referring to.

"Thank goodness," Lori's relief was obvious.

"I didn't realise that Ivan Delgado was engaged." Emma heard herself speak.

"Oh! Do you know Ivan?" Lori seemed genuinely interested that someone else would know Ivan, not acting the least bit jealous, unlike Emma, whose throat had turned to sand.

"He's a very popular doctor," Emma spoke, trying to act as normal as possible, despite the very real possibility that she was having a panic attack.

"I'm glad he seems to be fitting in here, he has been a bit lost, a bit out of sorts since he returned from overseas." Lori mused. Emma's chest ached, it was clear in the way that Lori spoke that she and Ivan shared a long history, something Ivan and Emma would never share. Emma knew she would replay this conversation in her head over and over again for years to come, but she had to know, she just had to.

"How long have you known Ivan?"

"All our lives, although, obviously, not romantically," Lori trilled. "We have only been engaged for a few months actually, that's why I am here, I thought it was about time we started to sort out our wedding plans, you would not believe just how far in advance you need to book everything these days!"

"I can imagine."

"Are you married...I'm sorry, I didn't even ask your name!"

"Emma, and no."

"Any kids?" Oh God, did she know? Could she tell? Emma studied her face but saw nothing other than genuine conversation.

"No, no kids. How about you?"

"No, I wanted to wait until I was married to start a family, but to be honest, I am not sure I even want kids. That's why Ivan and I are such a great match, he doesn't want kids either, we are both far too committed to our careers to have enough time or energy left over for children."

"Oh. Well." Emma really had no idea what to say about that. Ivan didn't want children, was that true? What was happening? Why was he insisting on being a part of her baby's life then, if he didn't want children? Worse yet, if his soon to be wife didn't want children. How would that child feel when they went over for visitations? Or maybe Ivan was not planning on that? maybe he knew it would not get that far, maybe he had planned the entire thing, intended to tell Emma just what she had wanted to hear in order to lure her into his bed. Emma's face flamed and she turned around quickly, not wanting Lori to see her, feigning busyness until she had her blush under control.

"Will Ivan be coming to meet you here?" Emma asked, desperately hoping not.

"No, he, ah, he doesn't know I am here. I mean, I didn't tell him I was arriving today, I wanted to surprise him."

"I bet you will."

"Is there a map in here?" Lori gestured to her accommodation pack.

"Yes," Emma nodded, "and whoever put it in there at the accommodation office will have highlighted your accommodation for you, so it should be fairly easy to find. If you are worried, I can get a security officer to show you there?"

"That would be great, thank you. I want to make sure that I have enough time to shower and fancy myself up a bit before Ivan gets home." Emma was desperate for this conversation to be over; she could feel bile rising up in her mouth at the very thought of Ivan being with Lori or her casual use of the word home. Security arrived promptly, helping Lori with her suitcases. Emma watched them in the cameras, like an outsider, someone window shopping, chatting and laughing all the way down the hall.

Emma picked up the telephone and dialled Ivan's number. No answer. She tried again. The telephone only rang out. Emma spent the next forty minutes trying to get through to Ivan without any luck. The more she tried to reach him, the more she felt cold inside. A dead, turn your bones to ice type of cold was seeping in, the longer her shift dragged on, the emptier she became. A shrill of the telephone shook her out of her gloomy thoughts, short-lived, as it was Lori on the other end.
"Emma?"
"Yes, Lori."
"Do you know where Ivan is? I mean, is he in theatre or..." she trailed off.
"No, I'm not sure sorry, would you like me to page him for you?"
"Yes please, can you page him to call me at this number, oh, but don't tell him it is me; can you do that?"
"Not a problem, already done," Emma confirms as she hits the send button.
"Thank you! I have to go; I have to put the champagne in the fridge." And with that Lori disconnected the call.

There was still no word from Ivan. Emma could only assume that he had called Lori back, as Lori had not called again asking Emma to page him. which meant what exactly? That he was glad to see Lori? That he was so stunned at seeing his fiancé that he forgot to call the switchboard and tell Emma that she was not welcome tonight? Was he carefully covering his tracks? Making up a story for Lori? How was he explaining her? How was he explaining the baby? Was he even trying to? Maybe he would just tell Lori that I had a crush on him, that the baby was not his? Would he do that? Emma would have said no, but now she was not so sure. Emma had asked him if he was married, and he had told her no. Granted, Emma had not specifically asked if he was engaged, but logic would follow that he would have admitted it if he was intent on being honest with her, which Emma was starting to realise, didn't seem likely.

She wondered what he was doing. Did he know Lori was here yet or was he still blissfully unaware? Had he seen her page? Called her? Made some excuse to his staff and rushed back to his unit, desperate to see Lori? Lori had told Emma that she had champagne in the fridge. Had it chilled? Did she put it in an ice bucket on the coffee table in Ivan's lounge room? Had she unpacked, mixing her clothes in with his? Emma was unable to stop the acidic train of her thoughts. Had Lori showered? Changed into something low cut and tight? Or had she just wrapped herself in a robe, for Ivan to unwrap? Perhaps she had not bothered, maybe she had merely arranged herself on Ivan's sofa, naked, waiting for him to get home. Emma was torturing herself with the images of Ivan and Lori together, by the time her co-worker arrived to relieve her, Emma was absolutely exhausted.

She tried paging Ivan one last, but there was still no answer. Emma knew that she should just go home, to the sanctuary of her bed, where she could sit and have a good cry uninterrupted and unseen, but instead of taking her in the direction of the car park, her traitorous feet carried her in the direction of the staff accommodation, Ivan's unit key a heavy weight in her pocket. As her feet dragged her closer, she thought about what she wanted to do. She won't make a scene, she promises herself, she won't make a fool of herself. Instead, she will simply knock on his door and ask him outright about Lori.

There was no answer to her knock, perhaps they were out? Emma stopped at the front door for a moment, contemplating her next move, before finally shoving her hand into her pocket and retrieving the key Ivan had left for her earlier. Oh, if only he had known then what he knew now, she very much doubted that he would have left her anything at all, let alone his unit key. Emma slid the key into the lock, it turned silently, and pushed the door open. She hesitated momentarily before stepping inside, grateful that there was no Lori arranged on Ivan's sofa, naked and waiting for him to get home. Emma walked through to the kitchen, placing the key in the middle of the kitchen bench, certain that Ivan would see it there. She could only hope that he would know what it meant, that Emma was done, that she knew about Lori and had decided to walk away head held high. As she turned back towards the front door, Emma froze, a soft noise coming from the bedroom. Laughter maybe?

Emma knew that she shouldn't, she really shouldn't, that nothing good ever came out of snooping, and yet she still turned down the short hall, coming to an abrupt stop in Ivan's bedroom doorway. There, standing in front of her was Lori, completely naked. She was, Emma decided, a goddess, perfection herself. Her blonde hair cascaded down her back, no blemishes or spots, no cellulite or chubby bits that she needed to hide or be worried about. Just utter perfection. And Ivan. Standing there, cupping Lori's face with such tenderness it made Emma's heart shatter. Their lips together, Emma knew that she couldn't take any more. She had not yet been seen, didn't want to be seen, not by Lori, who seemed not to know about Ivan's wandering hands, and not by Ivan, who would certainly only hurt her more. She let herself out of Ivan's unit, quietly shutting the door behind her, tears blinding her eyes.

Somehow Emma made it back through the hospital and out to her car, sliding in and locking the doors behind her. Lori had been telling Emma the truth, Lori and Ivan were engaged. A part of Emma had hoped that Lori was manipulating her. Emma didn't know how long she sat there, unable to move, paralysed by her grief, unable to stop the images that bombarded her mind. Ivan was kissing Lori, Emma was not stupid, she knew what would come next. Ivan would croon sweet words to her about how beautiful she was and how much he loved her, and Lori would undress him. Would he make love to her, slowly, sweetly? Or would he merely pound into her as he had with Emma? No emotions involved, pure lust and longing and sex? Both scenarios had Emma's body shaking with sobs, she wrapped her arms around her middle, feeling as if she might actually be breaking apart, as if she might need to genuinely hold herself together.

She couldn't believe that Ivan had lied to her. Emma would never have ever slept with Ivan had she known that he was engaged. Maybe that was why he had not told her? Emma was not a homewrecker, she was not a floozy, she didn't go around flirting and sleeping with men who were already taken. Heck, Ivan knew that, he knew that she had been a virgin, Emma didn't go around flirting and sleeping with anyone. Nor would she again her heart whispered. She would just make do, she would just pretend that it didn't hurt, that she didn't care. She could do that, couldn't she? After all, now that Lori was here, it was not as if Emma would be seeing Ivan again in a hurry. Lori had said it herself, neither she nor Ivan wanted children. There would be no reason for Ivan to see Emma again. Emma placed a hand on her abdomen, she wondered what would happen with their baby. Would Ivan still want to be a part of his or her life? Or was that just another one of his lies, said with the sole intent to get Emma into his bed? Emma wondered just how long he had been planning this. Was that why he had taken her to Brisbane? Had he hoped that would be the start of their sexual relationship?

Looking back, Emma could see that everything that Ivan had done was all an illusion. The expensive sports car, the penthouse, the sob story about his beach house, the way he had helped her around the house, all of it was one big giant lie. Had he planned this entire thing all along? Emma remembered that the first time they kissed, it had been Ivan who started it, the day he told her that she was indeed pregnant. He had kept telling her that it was his child that she was carrying, his child growing inside of her. Is that how he saw her? As a vessel? A possession? Is that what this baby was to him? His genetically, therefore his to possess, to own? But he doesn't want kids, Emma reminded herself, Lori had told her so herself. Emma was so confused. She was so embarrassed. She was so thankful that she had yet to tell anyone of her pregnancy, so glad that no one had yet to guess just how close she and Ivan had become. Outside of her doctor, and Ivan, no one else knew she was pregnant, and even her doctor didn't know who the father of the baby was, nor would he ever be informed.

Emma didn't know what to do, her head just kept repeating the same mantra over and over again. He lied to me, he lied to me, he lied to me. Ivan had lied, without reservation, straight to Emma's face. She didn't think there was any other time that she had felt so utterly betrayed. Nor so ashamed. When she thought of what it was that she and Ivan had done, she wanted to die of the guilt of it all. She had no idea how she would be able to face Lori at switchboard after this, whether she knew or not made no difference, Emma knew. Drawing in a ragged breath, Emma wiped her eyes with the heel of her hand, reaching across to open her glove box and rummage around for a tissue, only managing to come up with a crumpled serviette. Making do, Emma had a firm blow of her nose, and feeling a little bit more composed, turned her key in the ignition. As she shifted into reverse, her telephone rang, and glancing at the passenger seat she saw Ivan's name flashing on the screen. Not likely, she thought. If he knew that she had seen him with Lori he would be over to her house in a flash, making sure that Emma would not be talking to Lori, spilling his dirty little secrets. There was no way that Emma wanted to see him, she had to get home before that could happen.

CHAPTER TWELVE

Emma drives home largely on autopilot, letting herself into the house and locking the door firmly behind her. She wanders through the house, turning on lights as she goes, flicking on the television set for some background noise. She went and changed out of her work clothes, too tired to even bother putting it in the washing, instead just dumping it in the laundry. She pulled on her favourite pair of track pants and a cotton tee shirt, her comfort combo. She made herself a strong cup of tea and rummaged around in the cupboard hoping for something, anything, chocolatey, settling for a long-forgotten packet of chocolate chip biscuits. As she moved to carry her snack out to the lounge room her telephone rang and she jumped, hot tea spilling over her hand.

"Hello." She snatched up the telephone, moving to the sink to pop her hand under cold running water.

"Emma?" Ivan. Hearing his voice made Emma's blood run cold, and she disconnected the call, leaving the telephone off the hook, silent for the rest of the evening.

When her mobile telephone rang moments later, she ignored it and let the call go straight to voicemail, checking after she heard the beep, just in case the call had been from someone else. It was not, it was Ivan again. She turned her mobile telephone off as well, leaving the offending device on the kitchen table. Emma was not at all surprised when she heard a call pull up outside a short while later, and heard knocking at the front door, knocking which she chose to ignore. Let him sweat. A few minutes later the knocking stopped, and she heard a car door opening and closing, and an engine starting up. With Ivan gone, Emma abandoned her snack and crawled into bed, uncaring that it was still only late afternoon. Who was she trying to fool? Herself? It was no use, she was not in an afternoon tea and television mood, she was in a crying herself to sleep from stress and a broken heart and scared about the future of her unborn baby kind of mood.

Emma had not slept a wink last night, she had merely laid awake in her bed, tossing and turning, and overthinking everything. She had always been especially good at that, overthinking. Finally, the clock on the bedside table reading three o'clock in the morning, Emma gave up, throwing off her sheet and getting out of bed. She padded through to the kitchen and made herself a nice strong cup of tea, sitting at the table with a notebook and pen, needing to write a list in order to help her sort this entire mess out. Once she had finished her cup of tea, Emma stood, determined, and went to get dressed. Half an hour later she pulled her car up in front of her parents' house, and sat, waiting for any sign of life. She could have used her house key and gone inside, but she didn't want to give them a heart attack or be whacked over the head by one of her dad's gold clubs. No, better to wait for them to wake and turn a light on.

Both of her parents were early risers and Emma found that she didn't need to wait long. With a sigh, she got out of her car and went to knock on their front door.

"Emma." To say that her dad was surprised to see her would be an understatement. "Good heavens, do you know what time it is?"

"Yes dad, but I needed to speak with you and mum."

"Well, okay then, would you like to come in?" He held the door open wide for her to pass through.

"Thanks." Emma brushed past him and waited while he shut the front door.

"Well," her dad started awkwardly, "your mum is in the kitchen, come on, let's go see about getting us both a nice cuppa hey?" Emma smiled, determined to at least try to make this a pleasant visit.

"Sounds great dad."

Emma's mum was equally as surprised to see Emma, but recovered quickly, shooing both her daughter and her husband over to the table to sit while she bustled about fixing everyone something to eat.

"Emma, will bacon and eggs be okay with you?"

"Actually, that sounds kind of great mum, thank you, I haven't had much of an appetite lately."

"You've not been sick, have you?" Her father asked, brows knitted together in concern.

"No, not exactly, I um..." Emma trailed off. "Actually, I came here because I wanted to tell you both something, to share some news. I'm sorry that I haven't been by sooner to tell you this, but to be honest I was not really sure how you would take it." Emma took a deep breath. "Mum, Dad, I'm pregnant." Emma beamed. "And before you ask, yes, it was a planned pregnancy, and yes, I am keeping the baby, and no, the father is not in the picture, I used an In Vitro Fertilization clinic when I flew to Brisbane earlier in the year."

Her parents looked at her, stunned, neither one blinking. It was her mother who broke the spell, letting out an ear-splitting whoop, before uncharacteristically throwing her arms around Emma in an actual hug.

"Oh Emma, I am so excited for you! Just think," she addressed her husband, "we're going to be grandparents. Nanna and poppy. No, grandma and grandpa. No, wait! Nanny and pappy."

"Never mind mum," Emma laughed, "you still have about another four months left to decide, I'm only halfway through the pregnancy."

"Oh Emma, I'm so happy for you, I hope you – Argh! The bacon!" Her mother dashed off to remove the now extra crispy bacon from the stovetop. "Oh, dear." She placed the burnt offerings in the dog's bowl and went to fetch more bacon from the fridge. "I hope you know how happy we are for you Emma, I know we haven't always been there the way you would have liked, the way you needed, but we really are so very happy for you."

"Why didn't you tell us you were thinking about undergoing In Vitro Fertilization Emma, we would have been happy to help with the costs, I know that can't have been cheap." Emma's dad asked.

"I didn't think you would approve," Emma answered honestly. She was tired of lies and deceit and people not saying what was on their minds, if this whole mess with Ivan had taught her anything, it was that honestly was paramount.

"We understand," her mother came to stand behind her father. "Our mistakes are just that, ours alone. In our defence we acted the way we did from love, we only ever wanted you to be happy, you and your sister. Maybe now, with a new life entering the family, we can all find a way to move forward? I know old habits are not easy to break, but if we all try maybe we can be successful?"

"I would really like that mum, I think I am going to need you, both of you, in the coming years."

"It was a brave thing you did Emma, In Vitro Fertilization, on your own. It shows guts and gumption." Her dad smiled. "I bet the little tacker will take after you in that respect."

"As long as they don't take after their father." Emma didn't even bother trying to hide her bitterness.

"Their father?" Her dad looked puzzled. "I thought you used In Vitro Fertilization?"

"I did. It's a long story dad."

"Well, seeing as how your mother had burnt the bacon for a second time," her dad gestured to the smoke billowing from the frying pan, "I'd say we have time." As her mother put on yet another batch of bacon, Emma explained as best she could, the entire saga of

Ivan, starting with the clinic mix up and ending with Lori, deliberately leaving out the more intimate activities. Her parents could fill in the blanks if they wanted to.

Emma finished the story just as her mother finally set a plate of bacon and eggs down in front of them.

"That's a tough one Emma," her mother agreed. "Do you love him?"

"Yes." Emma didn't hesitate, she knew it was true, that she had stupidly allowed herself to fall in love with Ivan, would most likely always love him on some level.

"Well," her father said, pragmatically, "there is only one thing to do. Go shopping."

"Dad."

"What? It helps your mum feel better, doesn't it darling?"

"Yes honey, you are right, it does. Actually, Emma, that is a great idea. There is not much to be bought here in Alice Springs, but why don't you and I, and Rosalind if she can't make it, take a trip down to Melbourne? We can stay in a fancy hotel, get a pampering spa treatment, shop in the city, ooh, it will be so much fun!" Emma had to admit, it did sound like fun, and they spent the rest of their visit talking about what they would buy and where they would stay.

By the time Emma got back home, she was feeling a little brighter. She felt better for sharing her news with her parents, and later with Rosalind on the telephone, and it was comforting for her to know that she would not be truly alone with her baby, that her family would be there, as much as they could, in their own way. The next task on her never-ending to-do list was to call her boss, a task Emma was dreading. In the end, though, she chickened out, sending an email instead, informing her boss that she was sick and would be away for the following two weeks and that a medical certificate would be forwarded on to her later today. She then rang her local medical centre and asked to speak with her regular general doctor, pleading her case to him over the telephone, in the hopes that he would be able to book her in for a home visit. Instead, he did one better, offering to do a telehealth consultant with her on the spot, and then agreeing to write her out a medical certificate for her to collect at any time today.

Knowing that Ivan would be busy in clinics all day today made leaving the house a little easier for Emma, there was no chance of him waiting outside to ambush her or to try to get her to talk to him. She took her time in town, collecting her medical certificate and then stopping off at the newsagency for a magazine on pregnancy and parenting. On a whim she stopped and bought a box of muffins from a local bakery, sneaking into work through the back entrance, feeling rather like a spy. She stopped off to see her boss, handing in the medical certificate and shocking her outrageously when she asked about applying for maternity leave. Her boss, with a reputation as being rather cold-hearted and uninterested, surprised Emma with a broad smile, even going as far as to hug her, expressing concern that the baby was doing well. Emma assured her that baby was fine, it was Emma that was struggling, and her boss happily showed Emma how to apply for the maternity leave using the internal web forms, suggesting instead that Emma might like to take a printed version home and complete them during her sick leave. Forms in hand, Emma popped her head into the switchboard office, waving at her colleagues as she set down the box of muffins.

After a few minutes, the frantic nature of the telephone calls died down a little and Emma was able to share her happy news.

"I'm pregnant!" Her announcement was met with a chorus of congratulations and cheers, and hugs all around, earning a few funny looks from passing staff members. Emma spent the next twenty minutes between calls briefly explaining that she would be away for the next couple of weeks, but that the baby was fine, Emma just needed a bit of a break. Her co-workers were surprised at Emma's use of In Vitro Fertilization, echoing her parents' thoughts that she was brave to be willingly heading into parenthood alone. Emma was peppered with questions about the baby's gender and whether or not she had been for her first scan yet. When Emma admitted that she had not thought to book it yet, they decided to take matters into their own hands, calling the imaging department directly and asking for the earliest possible appointment. Booked in for three days' time, Emma was excited at the prospect of seeing her baby, promising to come straight back to switchboard afterwards and let the girls all know what the sonographer had said.

As Emma was about to take her leave, Lori appeared at the switchboard window. Emma slunk even further back into the corner, hoping that Lori would not see her there, shame building up inside of her. God, did she know? Had Ivan told her? Had he told her where he was going yesterday or had he lied to her as easily as he had lied to Emma? Emma snuck a peek at Lori, she looked happy, with no traces of a sleepless night, no puffy eyes from crying. She strained to hear what Lori was saying over the ever-ringing switchboard.

"Is Emma working today?" Emma's colleague shot her a look, pretending to glance at the roster, a question in her eyes. Emma shook her head no.

"I'm sorry, no. I believe she has a few days off."

"Oh, that's a shame, I thought I heard her voice as I passed by before, I really wanted to speak with her."

"She popped in briefly." Her colleague confirmed. "I would be happy to leave her a message if you like?"

"If you can, please. Can you please let her know that Lori Masters stopped by, she was a big help to me when I arrived yesterday, and I really appreciate it. She was kind when she didn't have to be, and I just wanted to say thank you, that's all."

"Okay," Emma's colleague wrote the message down. "I'll let her know when I see her next." With Lori gone, Emma came out from the corner, designed to be hidden from view, and used regularly when switchboard staff needed to eat between calls. Her colleague passed the note over to Emma who promptly screwed it up and threw it into the bin. At her colleague's questioning look Emma merely shrugged.

"Just don't ask." She muttered. Maybe one day, when it didn't hurt, she would confide in her, but for now, Emma could barely think the words, let alone say them out loud. "Look, I'm going to go, I'll see you all after my scan." She smiled, heading for the door. If she didn't get out of here soon, she was going to be sick. Lori had seemed happy enough, which meant that she either must not have been told where Ivan was yesterday afternoon, or he had actually told her, and she was okay with it. Had he told her about the baby? Kept things professional? Had she told him that she was going to the switchboard to speak with her? Emma could only imagine. Either way, she had to leave now, before she had the chance to run into Ivan.

Opening the back door, Emma spotted a group of doctors huddled together, Lori included, all writing notes furiously, dictated by Ivan. Huh. So, Lori was on his team, that was certainly going to be cosy for the two of them. Emma took half a step backwards, intending to hide like the coward that she was inside the back section of the switchboard until Ivan's group of doctors moved on to their next patient, but Ivan chose that moment to look up, his eyes meeting hers in an explosion of recognition. Emma couldn't have looked away if her life depended upon it, she was fixated on his gaze, every single thing he had ever said, every single thing they had ever done together, floated through her mind at once, a cacophony of sights and sounds and smells, making Emma dizzy with the emotion of it all. Suddenly scared, Emma was saved by the buzzing of everyone's pagers at once, meaning only one thing, a code blue had been called, summoning all senior doctors and their second in charge. Seizing her chance, Emma bolted for the hospital doors, making a run for her car, squeezing in, and locking the doors moments before Lori appeared at the hospital doors, scanning the carpark for Emma.

Shaking violently, Emma managed to drive home, locking herself in and collapsing on the couch, sobs wracking her body. She would never have to see him again; she reminded her broken heart. He didn't live here; he was only on a short-term contract like the rest of the staff at the hospital. Now that Lori was here, they would be far too busy to bother or annoy Emma, at least she hoped that would be the case. Maybe with Lori here Ivan would remember what Brisbane had to offer him, and move back sooner? Emma knew it was most likely wishful thinking on her behalf, while he might be a liar and a cheat, Ivan did genuinely seem to be interested in his patients and making the world a better place for those residents less fortunate than himself, something the residents of Alice Springs desperately needed in their trauma surgeon. She had no idea how she was going to do it, but Emma knew that she would need to find a way to work alongside Ivan, or at the very least, learn how to be civil to him while she was at work. The last thing she wanted was anyone lodging a complaint against her, and she couldn't quit her job, no matter how much she wanted to, she needed the money, especially now that she was pregnant.

With her sobs finally subsiding, Emma became aware of the fact that her telephone was ringing.

"Hello?" Her voice was hoarse, the word barely scratched out of her aching throat.

"Emma?" Ivan. Emma slammed the telephone down, the receiver echoing in protest. How dare he call her, after she blatantly ignored him at the hospital, after she gave him such an easy way out. She continued to ignore the ringing of her telephone for the rest of the night, getting to the point where she almost didn't recognise the ringing for what it was. Switching her mobile telephone to silent, she sent off a quick text message to her parents to let them know that her house telephone was currently not working, and they could reach her via text. Her mother then sent Emma a copious amount of text messages, each one discussing their planned trip to Melbourne. Despite everything that was happening with Ivan right now, Emma was really looking forward to getting away. She had been doing some research of her own online and had found the perfect little baby store in inner Melbourne that she just had to visit. As Emma's telephone lullabied her to sleep, she was stuck with overwhelming gratitude that she had not yet given Ivan a key to her house.

Emma woke to the shrill ringing of the telephone and forgetting why she was meant to be letting it ring out, she snatched it up, offering a sleepy greeting as she did.

"Hello," she mumbled, stifling a yawn.

"Would you care to tell me just exactly why it is that you are avoiding me!?"

"Ivan."

"Well. I'm waiting." An angry Ivan was not something that Emma wanted to face first thing in the morning, or at all if she was being honest with herself, so she once again hung up on him. The pounding on the door was inevitable really, and Emma opened it slowly, cautiously, keeping the chain firmly on. If Ivan wanted to yell at her, he would have to do it through the smallest of gaps.

"Ivan." She greeted him coolly.

"Emma." Ivan eyed her up and down, taking her all in before speaking again. "Open up and let me in."

"No."

"No? What do you mean no?"

"I mean, I'm not in the mood for your stupid games Ivan. Go away and leave me alone."

"I'm not going anywhere Emma, not until you explain to me just why exactly you have been avoiding me. I missed you the other night, I thought you were stopping by, yet surprise surprise, when I got home you had not only been there, but you had left the key there as well. Why? Emma, I thought we had a connection."

"Are you being serious right now Ivan? A connection, really? Is that what you are calling it?"

"Emma, are you okay? Is something wrong? Did something happen?" Ivan paled. "Emma, I didn't hurt you, did I?"

"No, Ivan, you didn't hurt me, not physically in any case." Regardless of how he had broken her heart, no man should ever be made to think that he had caused physical damage when he had not.

"Emma, please, I'm begging you, please tell me what is going on."

"You are such a good actor Ivan, even now," Emma didn't bother trying to hide the bitterness in her voice, she no longer cared if Ivan knew she was livid or not, let him know just how much pain he had caused her. "You always know exactly what to say, don't you, to get your own way. Well, it was a wasted trip, you coming here. I have no intention of telling anyone about us, I'll keep your dirty little secret for you, Ivan."

"Emma what the hell are you talking about!?"

"How many more have there been Ivan? Five? Twenty? You are overseas a lot, tell me, do you have a girl in every hospital? Is that how you operate, how you get through the day? Was anything you ever said to me the truth Ivan or was it all a lie?" The tears were falling freely down Emma's ashen face now.

"Emma ple-".

"Stop talking Ivan, seriously, just stop. I cannot bear to hear your voice anymore. Did she know Ivan? Did you tell her? Did the two of you sit in bed talking about that silly girl from the switchboard? Did you laugh about it, about me?" Emma was vaguely aware of the fact that she sounded hysterical. She was gasping for breath, trying to speak through her tears.

"I didn't return your key while you were out Ivan." She wrapped her arms around her middle, breaking open, trying to hold herself together. "You were there, in your bedroom with Lori, kissing her while she was naked. You see, I gave her the accommodation pack, she told me everything, that the two of you are engaged, that you do not want children. You didn't return my pages or telephone calls, so I went to confront you. I guess I got what I deserved, didn't I? Stupid, stupid me. I should never have trusted you; I should never have allowed you anywhere me or my baby."

"Emma, no! That's not-" Ivan's face was drained of all colour, ashen.

"Goodbye, Ivan." Emma sobbed, slamming the door and sinking down in front of it, curling up into a ball while her heart shattered into a million pieces around her. She could hear Ivan banging on the door, begging her to let him in, begging her to let him explain, but she couldn't move, so paralysed with grief. At some point she roused herself enough to move to her bedroom, climbing into bed fully clothed, where she remained for the rest of the day.

When Emma woke in the middle of the night after a horrid nightmare in which Ivan had shown up in the labour ward of the hospital and taken her baby out of his crib next to her bed and handed it to a laughing Lori, she knew something had to be done. The following morning, she called her parents and asked for the name of their lawyer, an hour later she was sitting in his office, a cup of tea in front of her and a pleasant-looking man seated opposite.

"Just so that I understand the situation, you wish to accept this man's original custody agreement, with a few minor alterations, even though, if we ended up in court, he would be unlikely to be granted as much, especially considering he concealed his engagement from you, and both he and his fiancé have both expressed a desire not to have children. Is that correct?"

"Yes."

"Miss Roberts, forgive me for being so blunt, but why would you agree to this?"

"Ivan is ruthless. Apart from being obscenely wealthy, he has the means to make my life hell." Emma confessed.

"Are you scared of him?" Daniel Burns had been the Roberts family lawyer for a number of years, and had grown quite fond of Emma and Rosalind, he hated to think of anyone bothering Emma.

"No," Emma answered truthfully. "If he pushed and pushed to the point where we ended up in court, he knows I don't have the means to fight him. If he is happy to support my baby, then so be it. If agreeing to this custody arrangement will get him out of my life, it will be worth it."

"Okay. What are the amendments you are seeking?"

"Firstly, Ivan is never to contact me. Not directly, not through family and friends, not through any work colleagues. The only way I wish for him to communicate with me is through my lawyer. I want both of our lawyers to always have the current address of where the other party resides, in case of an emergency. When the baby is old enough, Ivan can, if he wishes, purchase a second telephone line for my house, which he can use whenever he pleases to call the child. He is not ever to contact me via telephone." Emma paused to think.

"I think that grandparents and extended family, on both sides, should be able to contact the child by telephone whenever they choose." Emma continued. "The child will remain with me for Christmas and birthdays. Ivan will have the child every second Easter and every second school holiday, at his expense. Ivan will not be permitted to take the child overseas without my consent, although I will agree to both parties being contacted in case of any medical issues or emergencies. If Ivan chooses, he can pay for the child's education, but where he attends school will be solely up to me. I will agree to let Ivan cover all medical and dental bills, but as far as him paying child support, forget it, I do not want his money. If he absolutely insists on paying child support, then it is to be paid into a trust account for the child, for them to access when they reach eighteen years old." Emma finished; she was sure that was all of the amendments that she needed. "Will you be able to send a copy of that straight to his lawyer? Their contact details are on that agreement."

"Certainly. I should be able to get this all finished and submitted to the family law court before the close of business today. I will send his lawyer a secure digital copy, and I will also add him to the notification list so that he will be automatically alerted when the order is approved by the courts. I will add you and your parents to that list too if you like?"

"Yes please, I would appreciate that. It will be one less thing for me to have to worry about." Reassured after her visit to the lawyers, Emma stopped off at her parents' house, keen to fill them in on just what was happening and craving a little company. Her parents didn't disappoint. They agreed that her amended agreement was more than fair and that they would never have been as generous. Over a nice cup of tea and some of her mother's yummy orange cake, Emma and her mother poured over the list that her mother had made. They were officially booked on the flight from Alice Springs to Melbourne on the weekend, staying at the Hyatt for five days. Her mother had booked them all in for massages and facials on the day of their arrival, and again on the day of their departure so that they would feel amazing. The more her mother talked about it, the more Emma started to look forward to it. Yes, she was desperately in need of this break.

After such a lovely afternoon, Emma was reluctant to return home, her parents insisting that she stay with them in the spare room for just as long as she wanted to. Her mother even went as far as to let Emma know that she was welcome to stay here for the remainder of her pregnancy if she wanted to, but Emma was not sure that was the best idea. In the end, the thought of being alone in her tiny house made the decision for her and she found herself spending the evening with her mother spoiling her, even going as far as to bring her a cup of tea in bed, something that Emma could certainly get used to. Before finally drifting off to sleep, Emma pulled out her mobile telephone and, with shaking hands, sent Ivan a text message. Brief and to the point, it simply read: You win Ivan. I signed the custody papers today; my lawyer has lodged them with the family court and your lawyer will receive a notification when it has been approved. You will be advised via your lawyer when the child is born. You are not ever to contact me again. Do not call me on the telephone. Do not email me. Do not come to my house. Do not text me. Unless I am the only person working at the switchboard, you are not even to talk to me at work, is that clear? Emma saw the little green dot next to her text message, signalling that Ivan had read it, and then she switched her phone off and cried herself to sleep.

Her mother insisted on taking Emma shopping the following day, to stock her up on all manner of groceries her mother deemed absolutely necessary for a woman who was pregnant. Emma was too tired to argue, she had slept badly, and woken with a dull ache in the middle of her lower back. Emma half-heartedly threw in a punnet of strawberries and a block of milk chocolate, but for the most part, she just trailed after her mother, who was very clearly a woman on a mission. Her mother organised for the groceries to be delivered later that afternoon, and then Emma and her mother went to a local coffee shop to meet Rosalind for a decadent morning tea. It had been a really nice morning, almost a mini-break for Emma, who reluctantly turned down her mother's invitation to lunch, instead, choosing to return home. As much as she had enjoyed ignoring her responsibilities for the past few hours, the reality was, they were still there, and she needed to face them and decide what she was going to do.

Unpacking the shopping, Emma simply opened cupboards and chucked things in, she would sort it all out another day when she was not so tired. Getting to the bottom of the bag, she was surprised to see a wrapped gift, the gold tag bearing her name. She unwrapped it carefully, tears pooling in her eyes when she saw what it was. A gorgeous pregnancy journal and planner, the inscription in the cover was from both Emma's mother and her sister, expressing their deep joy and excitement. Emma took it over to the sofa, and sat, studying each page carefully. It was full of journaling prompts and spaces for photographs. Pages to record weird dreams and pregnancy milestones, places to write down fears and hopes. At the bottom of each page was a tiny little picture showing you how big the baby was for that week. Laying it on the coffee table, Emma thought about what she would put in there first. Maybe her first scan, which was happening tomorrow. A slow smile spread across her face. She couldn't wait to meet this little one, to actually see them on the screen, to have their first actual photograph to ooh and aah over with everyone. She wondered if it was a boy or girl. Secretly, Emma thought that she wanted a boy first, but she knew that she would love this baby no matter what.

As she lay back on the sofa, daydreaming about her baby, Emma realised that she had never been more exhausted in her entire life; she was sure of it. The past couple of days were starting to take their toll on her, the stress of avoiding Ivan at every turn, of worrying about her job, was all a bit too much right now. She just wanted to sleep. Despite it still being early in the day, not even lunchtime, Emma decided a quick nap on the sofa would do her the world of good. She flicked through the television channels until she found a repeat of one of her favourite television shows, snuggled under the quilt that usually hung over the back of the sofa, and promptly fell sound asleep. By the time Emma finally woke up it was almost three o'clock in the afternoon, and her back was aching something fierce. Standing, ignoring the twinges from her back, she stretched gingerly. She really needed to get a new sofa; this one had definitely seen better days. There was no way she would be able to breastfeed a baby on that sofa.

Padding through to the bathroom, Emma turned on the shower taps, letting steam fill up the room, undressing herself slowly, looking for any changes in her body. She luxuriated in the shower, the new shampoo and conditioner that her mother had purchased yesterday in the shopping smelt of honeysuckle and summer nights, the matching body wash divine. Emma even took the time to shave her legs, something that she had not done in over a week now. Finally, with the hot water tank drained, Emma stood wrapped in a thick, plush bath towel, feeling brighter than she had in days. She had not heard from Ivan since she had sent him that text message, and as much as she hated herself for this, she was feeling upset, bereft, that he had not tried to at least talk to her. How messed up was that?! Did he really have no feelings at all for her? Had he ever felt anything for her, other than uncontrolled lust? As she pulled on another pair of track pants and a tee-shirt, she reminded herself that she was pregnant and that it was most likely just the hormones making her act this way.

Knowing Emma as well as she did, along with the insane number of fruits and vegetables her mother had bought at the shops, her mother had also purchased banana ice cream and frozen pizzas, it was the latter that Emma now hunted for in her deep freezer, triumphantly holding it aloft like a sporting cup when she finally located it, eagerly putting it in the oven to cook. She paired her pizza with a sappy, comedic movie that followed a bunch of couples trying to fall pregnant, which was surprisingly fun to watch. With the credits rolling, Emma stood and rubbed her back. It had gone from a dull ache earlier in the day to an all-out constant throbbing. Pushing the discomfort aside, Emma headed to the bathroom, with what she suspected was the start of the curse of the pregnancy bladder, needing to find a bathroom frequently. As far as side effects went, this one was far preferable to the constant unrelenting morning sickness that she had suffered with earlier in the pregnancy.

As Emma sat down on the toilet, she saw something that made her heart stop. She was bleeding. No, no, no, she couldn't lose this baby, not now, not when she had fought so hard and so long to have them. Emma froze, she couldn't breathe, tears clouded her vision, racing down her cheeks as sobs tore from her chest, shoulders shaking. She couldn't think straight. She finished in the bathroom and went straight to the kitchen telephone, dialling a number she knew by heart.

"Switchboard."

"Can you put me through to maternity please?" Emma tried to keep the fear out of her voice, she didn't want her colleagues worrying over her. When the maternity ward finally answered Emma explained that she was bleeding, a lot, and they advised her not to worry, but to come straight down to the emergency department where they would meet her. Next, Emma rang her parents, who insisted on driving her to the hospital themselves. Emma waited outside in the fading twilight for them, tears falling down her cheeks, arms wrapped around her middle, marvelling in the poetry of another day fading just as her baby was fading too.

Emma's mother was frantic, rushing her husband out of the house, urging him to drive faster on their way to Emma's house. He didn't understand, he didn't know, what it was like, to lose a baby, to suffer a miscarriage, to lose something that you had so longed for and that had been so precious, and to be so utterly alone while it happened. But she did. Before they had been blessed with Emma, she had been pregnant. It was early days, and she had taken the test alone, her husband being away at work. She had nurtured her little secret, determined to tell him when they were together, face to face, she had wanted to see his face light up when he heard the news. She had never got that chance. A week before he was due to fly back home, she had awoken to terrible cramping, the pain knocking her off her feet. She lost the baby, sobbing and alone, on the cold bathroom floor. The doctor confirmed it the following day, although telling her pleasantly enough that she could go on to have more children, as if that had mattered.

Right at that moment, she had not wanted more children, she had only wanted that one. Her doctor had told her not to be hysterical, to think of her husband, and she had. A week later when he returned from work, she was acting like her normal self again. She had never told him, she didn't see the point, he was not able to do anything, he couldn't have fixed it, he would only have worried. It was the only secret that she had kept from him throughout their entire marriage. She saw though, the damage that it had done. When Emma had come along, she had not connected to the pregnancy, convinced that she would also lose this one. She had not fallen instantly in love with Emma, still longing for the baby that should have been, that never could have lived. She saw now, how that damaged her relationship with Emma, grateful that she was being given this new chance, to do it right, to be the mother that she should always have been. While Emma was being helped into the car by her dad, her mother had a quick look around the house, finding Emma's phone and pocketing it.

There was no way she would let her daughter go through this alone, not if she could do anything about it. No, she would find this man she so obviously loved, and let him know what was happening. If nothing else, he owed it to Emma to be there for her now, no matter what it was that he did wrong. Sliding in beside Emma on the backseat she looked over at her daughter at saw herself all those years ago, trying to hold on, trying not to fall apart, all the while knowing, as only a mother can, that real love is also real loss and real pain. She ached to hold Emma close, to tell her that everything would be all right, but the truth was, she just didn't know. All she could do was to be there for her daughter now, knowing how much she had longed for this baby, how much she would mourn if she lost it. Truthfully, she doubted that Emma would ever fully recover if the worst happened, if this bleeding was, in fact, a sign that the baby had passed away. Taking Emma's hand in her own, squeezing lightly, she only hoped that Emma knew how much she was loved, how many people she had in her life to support her through this, how many people would be willing to listen, if Emma ever needed to talk.

As they drove through the streets towards the hospital, life went on around them. Kids kicked a soccer ball in the park, a group of people, friends maybe, laughed as they sat outside a fast-food restaurant, card honked at the lights, keen to get moving. Emma saw none of this, her eyes unfocused on the chubby face of a toddler, dimpled cheeks and a toothy smile, holding a wildflower out to her in his chubby hand. Her most treasured dream now seemed a lifetime away. It was a tense and quiet ride to the hospital.

CHAPTER THIRTEEN

Her father pulled into the first available parking spot, leaping from the car to go and commandeer a wheelchair. Emma's mother remained in the back seat with her, holding her hand, silent, knowing there were no words that would make her feel better right now, only company and love. After what felt like forever, her father appeared beside the car, and Emma got out slowly, sitting in the proffered wheelchair, her whole body shaking. She was so cold, not even sure that she could feel her fingers or toes anymore. Why was she so cold, was that normal? Emma's mother told them to go ahead, she just needed to check something first, but that she would catch up with them in a few minutes.

Once she saw her husband and daughter inside the emergency department, Emma's mother pulled out Emma's phone and turned it on, relieved to see that there was no annoying passcode on there. Once on, Emma's phone played a lengthy tune of beeps and blurps, messages and missed calls lighting up the screen. With the exception of one of them, they were all from a contact named Ivan. On a hunch she hit the recall button, crossing her fingers as she did so, hoping that he would answer.

"Emma! Thank hea-".

"No, this is Emma's mother, Anne." She quickly interrupted. "I don't have time to be polite, I'm afraid. Are you my grandchild's father?"

"Yes." There was no hesitation.

"Okay then. I do not know what it was that you did to hurt Emma so viciously, but I also don't really care that much right now. Emma needs you, she is in the emergency department of the hospital, she's bleeding, a lot." Anne's only answer was a gasp and the sound of the call being disconnected.

Emma's father explained to the triage nurse what was happening, and they asked Emma to come right through, leading her down through the emergency department to a special section dedicated to maternity and genealogical patients. The nurse motioned for Emma's father to stay outside, and then she drew the curtains.

"Come on precious, let's get you up into bed, okay?" The nurse didn't wait for an answer, instead, she bustled about, turning down the sheets and helping Emma up out of the wheelchair and up onto the bed. "Shh, there you go precious. Let us get you warmed up; you must be freezing!" Emma was enveloped in warmth, the blankets stored in a heated cupboard. A box of tissues appeared at her bedside table, and the kind nurse patted her hand gently. "Please try not to worry precious. There are a lot of reasons for bleeding during pregnancy, not all of them are negative or serious. It is important to stay calm for the baby, okay?" Emma nodded. "Can I call anybody for you? Your parents are here, but did you want the father here too?"

"No." Emma shook her head. "He doesn't want me," her voice sounded so small, even to her own ears. "He lied to me; he's already engaged to be married."

"I'm so sorry precious, that must be very painful for you."

"I can't lose this baby, it's all I have left of him." Emma closed her eyes as sobs overtook her again. She heard the curtains slide open and felt strong arms encircle her, lifting her up off of the pillow and up against a strong chest. Ivan! His smell invaded her nostrils, she could hear his heart pounding, racing, through his shirt, currently getting soggy with her tears.

"Emma," his voice sounded croaky, cracked, strained with emotion. "Don't say that, please don't say that. You must know that it isn't true, you must know that you have me, Emma, please." Emma clung to Ivan, not caring how it looked, not caring how weak it made her.

"I can't lose this baby, Ivan. I just can't."

"Hush, it's okay, it will be okay, I'm here, it's okay." He stroked her hair away from her face, mopping up her tears with his thumbs. Emma knew that she must look a horrid mess, that Ivan must think she was overly emotional, but she was unable to stop the tears that fell. They fell for Ivan, for the man that she had fallen in love with. They fell for her baby, and the adventures she would miss. Most of all they fell for her, having loved Ivan and longed for this baby as much as she had, Emma knew that no matter what, she would never love anyone else. Ivan could throw a million barbs at her, could slice her open with his hurtful actions and hateful words, and her heart would still beat for him. "Hush sweetheart, I'm here. The doctor will be here soon, they'll run some tests, we don't know anything for sure, okay, nothing is certain yet." Emma merely nodded, remembering the blood that stained her underwear, her heart growing even more numb.

The nurse smiled comfortingly, adding another blanket to Emma's bed.

"Now your partner is here, I'll just pop out and make everyone a nice cup of tea. Did you want me to let your parents in yet Emma?"

"No, thank you." Emma chose to ignore the remark about Ivan being her partner. "I don't want to see anyone, not now, not until..." she trailed off.

"We understand, I'll let them know there is a family waiting room just down the hall, if they would like to, they can wait there, I'll come and get them if you need them." She stepped out of the cubicle, pulling the curtain shut behind her. Emma could hear her talking in low tones to her parents, heard the squeak of plastic chairs on hospital tiles, footsteps fading down the hall. She was alone. Just her and Ivan and a gulf of empty dreams and regrets between them. Emma didn't have the heart to correct the nurse, to scream that Ivan was not her partner, that he had never been. She had wanted to refute her, to tell her that Ivan meant nothing to her, but Emma knew the words were a lie, and they had withered to dust on her sandpaper tongue.

Ivan shifted his weight, turning slightly to sit on the bed facing Emma. Emma pushed away from Ivan and sat, studying him through wet eyelashes. He really was the most handsome man she had ever seen. She laid back against the pillow, closing her eyes briefly, imaging that the nurse had been right, that Ivan was her partner. In the ten minutes that they waited for the doctor; Emma imagined it all. She saw her and Ivan living together, sharing the mundane everyday things that couples share. She saw their children, rambunctious and kind, with the fair skin of their mother and the eyes of their father. She saw large, shared birthdays and laughter filled celebrations. She saw two heritages and two families blend seamlessly. She saw the fights and the making up. With the doctor's arrival also came her bleak reality. Ivan was not hers, she reminded herself sternly, he never was.

The doctor was kind enough, asking Emma about her dates, and once satisfied that they were all correct, he told her that he would arrange for an ultrasound to be done, at which point he would be listening for a heartbeat. He would not discuss anything further with Emma, preferring to do the ultrasound first.

"I'll just do a quick exam first, and then we'll arrange the ultrasound." Ivan stood up and headed towards the curtain.

"Ivan." Emma panicked. "Don't leave me!" Ivan stilled.

"I was just going to wait on the other side of the curtain, I thought you would like some privacy, but I can stay if you want me to."

"Please, stay with me." Ivan nodded, taking the chair next to Emma's bed, holding her hand fast in his own. Exam over, the doctor made a few notes in her chart, then left, promising to return in a few minutes with the portable ultrasound machine.

"I was booked in to have an ultrasound tomorrow," Emma spoke softly. "I was going to find out the sex of the baby, I wanted to go shopping with mum next week, and start decorating their room." A soft sigh escaped. "Now I might not get that chance." The thought set off more tears, quietly falling down her cheeks, shoulders shaking.

"Emma, oh darling, please don't worry, there is still hope." Ivan stood and crossed to her bed, shifting her over so that he could actually sit on the bed next to her. He pulled her across, onto his chest, and wrapped his arms around her, holding her, anchoring her. "There are a lot of reasons you could be bleeding, you heard what the nurse said, they are not all serious, they don't all indicate a pregnancy loss."

"I just wanted your baby, our baby, so much." Emma balls his shirt up in her fist, throat raw. She hears Ivan's gasp of surprise at her admission and buries in even closer to him. Even now, she couldn't get close enough to him, her traitorous body reacting to being so close to him again, the nipples on her aching breasts pebbling in anticipation.

"I know darling, I wanted it too."

"Why are you calling me darling?" Emma changed the subject.

"Emma, I thought, I mean, well, I thought that you knew, you are my darling." Emma remained quiet. She knew that Ivan was lying to her, she knew that he was engaged to Lori, that calling her darling was only to keep her calm, and yet she enjoyed it. She relished it. She committed the word to her heart, the sound of him saying it to her so that she would never forget. She knew that later she would torture herself with it, replaying it again and again, imaging him saying it just once more.

"Why are you here?"

"You need me." His answer was simple enough and yet somehow honest.

"I mean, how are you here, how did you know I was here?"

"Your mum called me on your mobile." That was interesting, Emma filed it away to think about later, shifting uncomfortably on the bed, a soft moan escaping her lips.

"Emma?" Ivan looked at her with worried eyes.

"Backache," she muttered, "since yesterday. I just can't get comfortable."

"Any other issues?" Ivan was in full doctor mode now; Emma could feel it.

"A little nausea, and..."

"And..." Ivan prompted.

"Some cramps." Emma's bottom lip wobbled. "It's bad, isn't it."

"We don't know that for sure, there is no point in worrying." At Emma's tears, he continued. "Oh, darling, come on, it will be okay, I don't want you to worry, I'm here now, I'm going to take care of everything. I promise, I'm going to take care of everything, I don't want you to worry." The doctor returned with the nurse, and they bustled around clearing space for the ultrasound machine.

With the ultrasound machine set up, the doctor asks Emma to lift her shirt, Ivan can see her hands shaking. Carefully, he moves her hands aside, taking her shirt in his own, folding it up carefully beneath her breasts. Next, he lowers the waistband of her tracksuit, tucking it up against her pubic bone. Ivan was struck with just how vulnerable Emma looked, trying to disappear into the bed, trying not to look at the ultrasound screen. Suddenly he couldn't stand it anymore. He had to tell her now, before things were too late.

"Doctor, wait," Ivan spoke. "I'd like a few minutes alone with Emma please, before we do the ultrasound."

"Okay, I'll go do a chart review and then pop back, in five minutes." Ivan was well known in the hospital as being a fine trauma surgeon, and a better man than most. Not one to pry, the doctor could only guess that this was Ivan's wife, and his heart was heavy with the burden he carried.

"Emma," Ivan covered her midriff with the blanket, "We need to talk, now, before it is too late."

"No, Ivan, we don't." Emma crossed her arms over her chest, turning her head away resolutely, refusing to look at him.

"Emma, please, Lori is-"

"How can you say that?" Was Emma's strangled reply. Eyes full of tears, stared at him, accused him. "How can you sit there while I am laying here, and say her name to me? Do you think I care about Lori?" Emma's words spewed from her mouth, laced with pain and acid. "Do you think that I care if you two are engaged? Sleeping together? What? Do you think that I'm going to tell her now, is that it? Do you think I am going to go running off to her crying about how you used me, about your nasty little affair while she was not around?" Emma drew in a shaky breath. "What would be the point, Ivan? Don't say her name, I don't want to hear it, I just want to go home."

"Emma, I'm sorry, but you have got to listen to me." Ivan moved up closer to her, leaning down low to speak into her ear. "I am not engaged. I am not married. I am not involved with anyone except you." Emma's heart fluttered; a tiny spark of hope flickered. "Only you." Ivan leant down and kissed her forehead, looking her directly in the eyes. "I have never been engaged, or married, I have never cohabited with anyone else either. Lori is the daughter of my mother's best friend, we have been friends since childhood, that is all we have ever been Emma, friends."

"Huh," Emma snorted. "It really looked like you were friends when she was naked in your arms, kissing you!" She gulped back another sob.

"Darling, I am so sorry that you saw that I really am, but if you had stayed-"

"If I had stayed! Are you seri-" Emma interrupted vehemently.

"If you had stayed," Ivan continued, "then you would have seen what happened next, you would not be torturing yourself so. You would have known that as soon as Lori started to kiss me, I took her by the shoulders and pushed her away, gently Emma, so as not to hurt or embarrass her further."

"I explained to her that while I was flattered, I was already taken." Ivan took Emma's hand once more, squeezing it tight. "By you Emma. Lori had no idea, Emma. My mother," Ivan shook his head, not sure if his relationship with this mother would be able to be saved, not if Emma lost their child, "told Lori's mother that I was ready to settle down, something that she has been scheming for years. I am so sorry Emma; I think our Brisbane trip inspired her in her mission to see me married off. Lori's mother assumed that my mother had been referring to Lori as my future wife. She then told Lori that I was ready to settle down with her, and promptly sent her here. Lori has been frantic Emma, she had no idea that I was involved with anyone, was unaware that she was merely a pawn in her mother's plans. She feels horrible Emma, and embarrassed, for kissing me, for throwing herself at me like that, but mostly Emma, she feels dreadful for telling you that she was my fiancé. She was trying the word out, harmless enough, until I told her that you were the woman I was involved with, the woman that I loved. I had no idea that you had seen that, Emma. If you had arrived a few minutes earlier, or later, we all would have laughed about the mix-up and had a wonderful dinner together." Ivan cupped her tear-streaked face in his hands.

"Emma, I love you. You are the one I intend to spend the rest of my life with, the only one I want. I have known it for weeks, I was just too scared to tell you, I didn't want to scare you away. It is why I took you to Brisbane, to the beach house. I wanted to show you what I was offering. A home. A family. A life together. I wanted you to see what I wanted in life, what I wanted to share with you. Oh, Emma, I longed to take you into my arms right then and there on that beach, to tell you what was in my heart, but I held my tongue. I thought that there would be plenty of time to tell you, to show you, how much I loved you. I think I first felt that spark with you the day you walked into that clinic and didn't cower to my demands. When you gave yourself to me the other night Emma, I thought, I had hoped, that it meant that you had feelings for me too. It was the best night of my life Emma, hands down. I love you Emma, baby or not, and that will never change. Will you please forgive me? Please, please forgive me my darling, please. Let me prove to you just how much I love you, I'll wait as long as it takes, please, just say you'll forgive me for ever hurting you."

"Ivan, no," Emma shook her head slowly, as if in a fog. "I can't forgive you."

"Emma." Ivan rasps, throat thick with pain. "Please."

"I can't forgive you, Ivan," Emma sits up, holding on to his shirt in her hands, "because there is nothing to forgive."

"Emma," with a groan he gathered her to him, lips meeting hers, gently at first, then more urgently, his tongue seeking entrance. Her fingers in his hair, she drew him closer, needing to feel him.

"Ivan," Emma reluctantly pulled away from his kiss, "seeing you with Lori broke my heart," Emma didn't bother trying to hide the way her voice cracked or the tears that fell. "It broke my heart Ivan, because I love you." She confessed, watching the way his face transformed with wonder. "I have loved you for weeks, I just didn't want to admit it to myself, or to you, I was so worried that it was just hormones, that you would not feel the same way, so I stayed quiet. Seeing you with Lori nearly killed me, I love you more than I knew was possible Ivan. It is you I love, you who owns my heart, for always." Emma ended her confession on a sob, the emotion of the day just too much for her to hold in any longer.

Ivan brought his mouth down to meet Emma's in a kiss full of lust and longing and raw need, only breaking apart reluctantly when they hear a polite cough from the returning doctor.

"Whatever happens Emma, we'll get through this together." Ivan clasps her hand tightly in his.

"Promise?"

"I promise." Ivan asserts, nodding at the doctor to begin the ultrasound, knowing that he and Emma would face whatever came together, always.

"Doctor," the doctor smiled at Ivan kindly, holding out the ultrasound doppler. "Would you like to do the honours?" Ivan looked to Emma, who nodded.

"Whatever happens Ivan, I want to hear it from you." The nurse helped Emma into position while Ivan warmed the gel, squirting it on her stomach and carefully smoothing it out.

"Are you ready Emma?" Ivan switched the ultrasound machine on.

"I'm ready." She nodded at him, the man she loved, the man she trusted with her life.

EPILOGUE

Their initial scare turned out to be nothing more serious than a slight tear in the wall of the uterus, easily fixed with bed rest. Ivan promptly moved into Emma's house and he and her mother drew up a schedule, ensuring that Emma would not be alone again during her pregnancy, neither one wanting to take any chances with the health of Emma or the baby. After their initial scare, Emma's pregnancy had continued along problem-free, and they were married as soon as they could arrange the licence. Cleared for travel, Ivan and Emma married at the beach house, the wedding had been a family and friends only affair, even Lori was invited, after all, Emma had informed Ivan when he asked if she was sure about her invitation, she had been responsible for bringing them together in the end.

Their days fell into a routine of sorts. Emma, having resigned from her job, spent her days with her mother, pottering around the house. While at first, she had found the inactivity tiring, Emma relished this quiet time with her mother, and the rest she was getting for her baby. Ivan spent his days at the hospital, calling Emma frequently, just to hear the sound of her voice. All of the switchboard staff were notified that any call from Emma or her parents were to be put straight through to his mobile. Their nights were just for Emma and Ivan. With her mother returned home to her father, Ivan would gather Emma into his arms, cooing softly to her stomach, telling their child all about his day and how proud he was of them for being a good baby for their mum. During dinner, Ivan would insist on hearing all about Emma's day, and every movement the baby had made. After dinner Ivan would lead her through to the bedroom, showing her with actions just how much he loved her and their baby, how much he loved their life.

Tonight was no different. With dinner finished and the dishes done, Ivan threw the tea towel onto the bench, smiling at Emma with undisguised love burning in his eyes. He stalked across the room towards her, slowly, until he stood in front of her, arms resting either side of her on the kitchen bench. Slowly, very slowly, he leant down, capturing Emma's mouth in a kiss that was so full of love and promise, it left her breathless and weak in the knees. He scooped her up, ignoring her protests of her being too large for him to do that now that she was at 39 weeks gestation, and carried her through to the bedroom. He stood her at the end of the bed, undressing her with reverence, kneeling before her to kiss her stomach. Emma knew that Ivan never tired of her, that he thought she was beautiful, that he adored watching her stomach grow rounder with their child, their expression of love, nestled in there, contentedly growing. Standing, Ivan stripped his clothes off, gathering Emma back in his arms and placing her carefully on the bed as if she were made of glass. She smiled up at him, growing hot, his gaze raking over her body, drinking her in, committing her to memory.

Ivan's hand slid down, gliding over Emma's stomach and down further, to cup her centre, growing hard at the discovery of her wetness, idly wondering if the day would ever come when he would tire of knowing that he made her that wet. With a sigh of contentment, he dipped his head to capture her breast, teasing her nipple until he felt it harden and pebble beneath his tongue, suckling and biting, loving the sounds it elicited from Emma. His fingers slipped further down, delving into her silky folds, dipping in and out with a leisurely speed, as Emma moaned and writhed beneath him. Releasing her swollen nipple, Ivan moved his attentions lower still, probing his tongue into her very core, teasing, tasting, drinking in her juices, as she bucked her hips beneath him, her breathing growing laboured. Helping her to her knees, Ivan guided her hips down to take him in, his hands glided down her sides, cupping her bottom and pressing her firmly against his erection. Emma moved her hips in small circles, her nub rubbing against Ivan's pelvic bone, teasing him slowly, gasping and jerking away from his mouth when his hand slipped in between them and gave her nub a hard tweak, shooting spasms of pleasure to her very core.

Even now, the feeling of being buried deep inside Emma, the way her walls felt as they stretched to accommodate his size, was enough to tip Ivan over the edge. She was mesmerising, he decided as he watched her arch her back, flinging her head back as she sang his name, taking him deeper still. He started to move inside her, his eyes feasting on the sight of her, hypnotised by the way her breasts swayed and danced for him as she met and rode every one of his thrusts. Emma screamed in pleasure as he drove in harder and deeper, his thick member filling her to breaking point, his pelvic bone pressing against her sensitive nub. She held nothing back as he moved within her, she was his completely. Ivan gave one final thrust all the way into her core and felt her walls tighten around his stiffened member as he pushed her over the edge, watched as she threw her head back in a scream of triumph as she orgasmed atop of him, bucking her hips as her release tore through her. Emma called his name, tipping him over the edge, as with one final thrust, he exploded inside her, gripping her hips for support as she ground down onto him until his spasms stopped, collapsing onto his chest with a contented sigh.

Ivan had never been more spent in his life, or more turned on. Every time with Emma was like the first time, an exciting mix of love and lust, trust and communication, discovery and shared experiences. It was Ivan's favourite part of the day, coming home to Emma, and one he intended on savouring for the rest of his life. As they held each other, they talked of their future plans, and discussed, yet again, baby names. When Ivan had performed Emma's ultrasound and detected a heartbeat, they had both cried with joy, hugging and clinging to each other. Ivan had decided that he didn't want to see any more, had asked the emergency department gynaecologist to finish the scan, not wanting to accidentally discover the baby's sex. As it turned out, their baby was shy, and the gynaecologist was unable to determine the gender. Since their scare, Ivan and Emma had been to three more ultrasound appointments, and their gynaecologist was still unable to determine the sex. Ivan and Emma were looking forward to the surprise.

They didn't need to wait much longer, Emma waking Ivan in the middle of that same night, their limbs still tangled together from lovemaking.

"Ivan." Emma shook him gently, then when he didn't respond, she shook him again, this time using more force.

"Mmhmm." Emma rolled her eyes at her husband, honestly!

"Ivan!" She shouted, more urgently, this time getting a response.

"What is it? What's wrong?" Ivan sat up and looked around the room.

"We need to go to the hospital." Emma moved to the edge of the bed, heaving herself up to her feet.

"Urgh, now. Why? It is two o'clock in the morning." Ivan rolled out of bed and picked up his pager, frowning when he saw no message there.

"It is the baby."

"What baby."

"Seriously Ivan," Emma couldn't keep the frustration out of her voice. "Our baby!"

"What?!" Ivan was by her side in a flash, his hand splayed across her abdomen, he was rewarded with a sharp kick and a tightening of the muscles beneath his hands. "How far apart are the contractions?"

"I don't know; I just woke up Ivan." Emma gestured to their bed. "My waters broke." As Emma moved to get dressed, Ivan stopped her, pulling her close and holding her in his arms, this would be the last time it was just the two of them. He released her and they both dressed, Ivan, helping Emma into the outfit she had chosen to wear to the hospital, collecting her birthing bag and her birth plan on the way through the house. His family would be so excited, they were due to arrive on the first flight from Brisbane later today, having planned to await the birth of their first grandchild, and then stay on to help Ivan and Emma for a few weeks, getting to know Emma's family in the process.

"Would you like me to call anyone yet?"

"No, I want to wait, just a little bit longer." She clutched his hand as a contraction hit, listening as he coached her through it. "I want to call your family when they are at Brisbane airport, so they know to come straight to the hospital when they arrive."

Which is what they did, and where Ivan found them, his parents and his brothers, along with Emma's parents and her sister, hours later when he left Emma's side at her urging, to stretch his legs. They all jumped up when they saw him, talking over each other, keen to know what was happening.

"No baby yet, but the doctor doesn't think it will be too much longer." He smiled; pride evident in his voice. "Emma is doing great; she is as fierce as a warrior."

"Do you need anything Ivan?" His father and he had grown a lot closer in the past few months, there was an understanding, a camaraderie that wasn't there before, a shared reality of marriage and fatherhood.

"Thank dad, I would kill for a proper coffee. If I give you the keys to my office, will you go and make me one, please? I would go myself, but I hate to leave Emma." Coffee was forgotten about as the nurse appeared in the hallway, summoning Ivan. Emma needed him.

Rubbing her back for her, having decided that he wanted the dad role more than the doctor role, he helped Emma to sit higher up, bracing her against his chest, her arms resting on his raised knees.

"Come on darling, just one more push, one more and we meet this little monkey." Ivan coaxed, excitement evident in his voice. Emma bore down as Ivan counted, resting on ten, exhausted. "Emma, the head is out, I can see them!" Ivan peered around Emma, desperate to see his baby. The gynaecologist smiled across at his nurse, there was always an extra layer of joy in helping to deliver a colleague's baby, even if they were from a different department. "Once more, once more Emma, come on darling, you can do this, I know you can, you are so brave, so fierce, you can do this." Ivan encouraged as Emma pushed, gripping her knees for support, Ivan holding her forearms. Her efforts were met with the shrill cry of a newborn, and a triumphant holler from Ivan.

"Emma, you did it! You did it! Listen to that cry, as fierce as you are." He beamed at his wife, waiting for the gynaecologist to finish his checks.

"Ivan, would you like to tell your wife the news?" Ivan looked to Emma, who nodded, then he climbed off the bed from behind her, moving to their baby while the nurse helped Emma into a more comfortable position. Ivan looked down, a grin spreading across his face.

"Emma," he held up their baby for her to see, "we have a son. I have a boy!" He wrapped their son in a blanket, uncaring of who saw him crying tears of joy and took him across to Emma, placing him carefully in her arms.

"A boy." Emma smiled down at the baby, enraptured, her finger gently tracing his little button nose. "It looks like he will have your dimple." She teased Ivan.

"So it does," Ivan had to agree. "Emma, thank you, for making our family, for our son. He is perfect."

Once Emma was presentable, she was keen for Ivan to show their families in, brushing away his concerns that she rest.

"Ivan I will rest later, I promise, but for now, I want our family to meet him." Reassured that Emma was feeling well enough for visitors, he strode out into the hallway, surprised to see a large number of his colleagues had joined their family in waiting for news.

"We have a son!" Ivan announced, the answering cheer that went up was heard by Emma in her bed. "He is perfection, and Emma is ready for you all to come and meet him." Ivan led the group back to Emma's room, where everyone fussed and oohed and aahed over both baby and Emma. There were hugs and handshakes, and much ribbing for Ivan from his older colleagues who had already been fathers and who were keen to welcome him into the club. As the baby was passed around for cuddles, flowers were delivered, and his father popped a bottle of celebratory champagne, to toast the happy family.

Later, when Ivan was alone with Emma and his son, he gazed down at his exhausted wife, his newborn son, Lucas, nuzzling at her breast, and he knew he was the luckiest man alive.

"Ivan." Emma rested her hand on his thigh.

"Yes, darling."

"Will you promise me something?" At this moment Ivan knew that he would have promised her anything.

"Name it."

"No more clinics," Emma looked up at him shyly. "Next time, I want to make our baby the fun way. I want to look into your eyes when I tell you that we are taking this crazy adventure again."

"Emma," Ivan groaned, full of longing. "I would be happy to take this adventure with you as many times as you want." Leaning down, he captured her mouth in a kiss, thanking his lucky stars for that original clinical error that brought Emma and his baby into his life.

THE END

Keep reading for an extract from "The Marriage Deal", "The Cynical Doctor's Christmas Wish", and "A Christmas Hope".

About The Author

An international bestselling and award-winning author of sweet contemporary romance, Kathleen's novels showcase thought-provoking plots and strong emotions that have been likened to a Hallmark movie. Featuring feisty heroines and strong heroes, where everyone gets a happily ever after. To discover more about Kathleen: Connect on social media

Read More of Kathleen's Books

The Flying Doctor's Christmas Wish
The Brooding Doctor's Christmas Wish
Christmas Wish Collection
The Surgeon's Baby
Fling With The Flying Doctor
The Marriage Deal
Caleb's Song
Cinnamon Kisses and Gingerbread Wishes

**Keep reading for an extract from
"The Marriage Deal".**

The Marriage Deal Extract

Millie left the building in a daze, her breath hitched, tears threatening to spill from her eyes. The main street of Maitland was bustling with people, as it always was on a Friday afternoon. Only three and a half hours drive from Sydney, it was a popular weekend getaway for a lot of city dwellers. When her grandfather had died, leaving her as the sole inheritor of the idyllic property that she had lived at since the age of thirteen, she had dreamed of turning it into a luxury wedding venue, a place where the bridal party could relax and refresh before the big day. A place where the ceremony and reception could be held, close enough to town for the wedding guests to travel without strain. Millie had even had a honeymoon cabin built onto the property, complete with a deck overlooking the lush property, perfect for relaxing in the outdoor spa or around the firepit. Unfortunately, as Millie was only just discovering, her grandfather had taken out a second, secret, mortgage on the property, which had now come due. Millie felt sick with the thought that she might be in danger of losing her home, her entire life was tied up in that property, every memory that she had ever made that was worth keeping, had been formed on that land.

There was no way that she was going to lose it without a fight.

First, though, she needed answers. And a plan. Millie wove her way through the throng of tourists, her feet taking a well-worn path, headed for The Daily Grind, a quaint coffee shop always overflowing with people and laughter. She slipped through the door marked STAFF ONLY and donned a frilly white apron from the shelf behind the counter, waving hello to her friend as she went. She knew this coffee shop like the back of her hand, it had been in the Capel family for over thirty years. The owner's daughter, Rachel, had taken Millie under her wing the first day she had met her, Millie's first day of high school, midway through the term. When the other girls had mocked Millie for having the wrong uniform, Rachel had defended her. They had been inseparable ever since. The rest of the Capel family had followed suit, and Millie had found herself surrounded by the love of a family, something that she had never known previously.

After high school the two friends had attended university together, choosing to travel each day rather than stay on campus, neither one wanting to have to leave Maitland. While Rachel had studied a Bachelor of Business, majoring in retail and management, Millie had studied a Bachelor of Communications, majoring in Event Management. Rachel had taken over the day to day running of the family business once she had graduated, something that Millie was always happy to help her with, without needing to be asked. Millie's plans of starting up her own event planning business had been put on hold once she graduated, instead of starting a new chapter in her life, she instead found herself having to say goodbye to a chapter of her life.

Her grandfather had suffered a stroke the weekend Millie graduated and required around the clock care, something she was honoured to provide, after everything that he had done for her. He never fully recovered, and eight months later he slipped away in his sleep. Millie would have been lost those first few months without her grandfather, had it not been for the Capel family. They felt her pain as if it were their own, adding her daily chores to their own load, never once commenting or complaining. It had been the hardest period of Millie's life, losing her grandfather. Even her brother, Joshua, having returned home on leave from the army, was unable to ease Millie's pain.

Millie had been thirteen and Joshua fifteen when they had come to live with their grandfather, following the death of their mother Caroline, in a car accident. It should have been tragic, but the truth was, Caroline had never been much of a mother, instead leaving Millie and Joshua to be raised by a bevy of nannies. Their father, Peter, Millie's grandfather's son, had died shortly before Millie's second birthday, and Caroline had wasted no time in marrying, and divorcing, a long line of men, each one richer than the last. Living with their grandfather had been the first stable home that Millie and Joshua had ever known.

A couple of weeks later, after laying their grandfather to rest, Millie and Joshua sat down and discussed the will and their plans for the future. Joshua supported Millie one hundred percent, having no doubt in her ability to both found and run, a successful wedding planning business. While their grandfather had left the house to Millie, he left the property to Joshua, and she was eager to have his support. In the end, they had decided that the best course of action would be for Millie to remain on the property and convert it into her idyllic wedding retreat venue, and for Joshua to return to the army to finish out his contract. Joshua's heart was never really in farming, he had always wanted to make a difference in the world, and he believed that he could do that by remaining in the army. They both knew that Tillie was never going to be a farmer either, which only left them with one other option, to lease the farm paddocks to someone else. Luckily for Joshua and Millie, the neighbouring farmer was looking for a way to increase his stock levels, and leasing their farm was the perfect solution for all involved.

Although Joshua returned to the army once everything was sorted out, he still returned every chance he got, being just as much tied up to Maitland as his sister was. He was due home at the end of the month, by which time Millie would have to either have an answer for the bank or be prepared to lose everything. Which is why she now found herself in The Daily Grind. If anyone would understand, would be able to help her to think of a solution, it would be

Rachel. It wasn't until almost two hours later that Millie finally got a chance to speak to Rachel. The lunch crowd had just started to thin out, their stomachs full of delicious pasties and delectable cakes. Millie sank gratefully into a vacant booth, smiling as Rachel appeared with a tray laden down with steaming mugs of hot coffee, and plates of homemade lasagne and garden salad.

"Millie thank you; I really appreciate the help." Rachel smiled at her friend. "It has been frantic around here today, with Mum off sick, and the tourists all here for the long weekend."

"You know you never have to thank me," Millie brushed her friend's comments aside, "it is my pleasure to help you, you know that."

"I do. So," Rachel quirked an eyebrow in Millie's direction, "what's wrong? You look like you have seen a ghost. Oh no, is it your mum, is she back to cause havoc?"

"No, it's my grandfather. I had a meeting with the bank manager today my grandfather took out a second mortgage on the property, shortly after Josh and I arrived in Maitland. The loan documents weren't in his will or with his personal papers, I had no idea it even existed." Millie took a large slug of her coffee, needing fortifying.

"If I had only known about it Rachel, I could have been paying it off, instead of letting it sit there. There haven't been any payments into that loan in years, and it has now come due. The new bank manager only recently got to the loans, he has been busy settling in, whatever that means in a town this size. The loan is due, in full, by the end of the month, or else I lose everything."

"No!" Rachel slapped her hand over her mouth, shaking. "How much do you need? We'll cover it, you can pay us back whenever, no matter how long it takes."

"You can't help Rach, it is too much." Millie shook her head.

"Name it." Rachel oozed confidence, something Millie had always envied her for.

"Two million dollars." Out loud, the amount seemed insurmountable. "It covers everything. The house and contents, the land, all the machinery, and the stock. I'll lose everything."

"Millie, I don't know what to say."

"All those things we had, everything we had ever wanted, we got. The horses, musical instruments we never learnt to play, a birthday event every year. I never even thought about where the money was coming from, it never even occurred to me. I just presumed that he had the money, that we were lucky, luckier than others in town, who we saw struggle each year. When I think about everything that he did for us, or got for us, or allowed us to experience, I just feel ill."

"What did Josh say?"

"I haven't spoken to him yet; he is on a training mission and not contactable until the end of the month."

"Oh Millie, we'll figure something out, we have to."

"I don't think that I have that many options, to be honest with you Rach. I could sell off the land in parcels, and just leave the acre around the house for Josh and I. I could sell off anything that we have of value, all my grandfather's antique furniture and paintings, the farming equipment and leftover stock, the horses too. But even then, I am not sure we would be able to raise enough in such a short amount of time. When I spoke to the bank manager today, I asked him for an extension, and he turned me down flat. He wants his money."

"I'll talk to mum and dad tonight; we'll ask around town. There must be something we can do, a charity concert or auction or fundraising event of some kind."

When Millie finally left Rachel's coffee shop, there was a slight chill in the air, and the sun was just dipping below the horizon. Nothing had been sorted out, but just talking to Rachel had made Millie feel a whole lot better. As she shifted her Ute into gear and pulled out of the parking lot, Millie gazed out of the window at all of the happy holidaymakers, without a care in the world. She had been overly confident in her abilities, thinking that she could turn her grandfather's property into a boutique wedding destination that brides would vie for, and now she was paying the price. Two million dollars was a lot of money, money that Millie could hardly imagine. Two million dollars was more money than she and Josh would earn, collectively, in their entire lives, she was sure of it. She sighed heavily. She didn't know anyone who had that kind of money. Well, unless you count the Marsden family, which Millie most certainly did not!

The Marsden family had been a part of Maitland since the year dot, Millie wasn't sure how many generations of their family had worked their land. They were revered around here, treated like royalty. Millie quite liked June Marsden and her husband Robert, they were kind to all they met. Their sons, however, were an entirely different matter. Jack Marsden was the youngest, Millie's age. She wasn't particularly close with him, as far as Millie knew, he was a pretty high flyer in Sydney, he hardly ever returned home to Maitland. Then there was Samuel, the elder brother. The same age as Josh, they had taken to each other the same way Rachel had taken to Millie. Samuel and Josh had been inseparable, much to Millie's chagrin. She had never liked Samuel, had always found him to be too sure of himself, too arrogant to be worthy of her time. He had been a firm friend to Josh though, was still his closest friend, and for that, Millie would always welcome him with politeness, even if they would never be close themselves.

As Millie continued her drive back to her grandfather's property, for in her head that is what it would always be, his, regardless of whose name was on the title deed, a seed of thought began to take shape. Once home, Millie slipped out of her going-out-in-public-and-need-to-make-a-good-impression-outfit, and into her everyday house clothes of leggings and a tee-shirt. Millie had never been one for fuss and bother, much preferring comfort over any form of style. Millie made herself a strong cup of coffee and took it through to the lounge room. She lit a fire in the fireplace, although it really was far too warm to need one, Millie found the flickering flames mesmerising and relaxing. She picked up a notebook and pen and started to jot down her idea. It was crazy really, maybe even bordering on insane. If it went badly, she would be laughed out of the house, she would never be able to look them in the eye again, would in all likelihood, need to move away from Maitland forever. Not that there would be a reason to stay, if this plan didn't work, she wouldn't have anywhere to stay, no place to call home, no venue to run her business, Blush Wedding Designs. She also ran the very real possibility of damaging her relationship with her brother.

She looked down at the paper in front of her. It was a major risk, she knew that. She had nothing to offer, yet everything to gain. This plan had to work, it had to, she could not fail at this, it was just far too important. Millie choked down her pride and nodded firmly, her mind made up. She would do it. First thing tomorrow morning she would go and ask to speak with him, she would beg if she had to, although she really hoped that she would not need to resort to such a tactic. If by some miracle, she did manage to raise enough money, or to borrow enough money, to cover her grandfather's bank loan, Millie still had the teensy weensy issue of how she would then manage to pay that loan back. A problem for another day, Millie decided, downing her remaining coffee in a single mouthful and standing. Right now, there were chores to be done before bed, and she would need to get a good night's sleep she was hoping to be able to pull off her audacious plan tomorrow morning. She would need time to prepare, to look the part. It would not be at all advantageous for her to go begging in her house clothes, evidence of a sleepless night showing beneath her eyes.

No, Millie squared her shoulders as she headed for the barn, tomorrow she would look as if she were dripping in money, no matter how long it took her to get ready in the morning. She would wear her best outfit, the one usually reserved for weddings. Tomorrow, it would be her battle armour. She was not going to lose her grandfather's farm, not without a fight.

**Keep reading for an extract from
"The Cynical Doctor's Christmas Wish".**

The Cynical Doctor's Christmas Wish Extract

Luca breathed deeply as he heard the bridal march begin to play, surreptitiously wiping his sweaty hands on the side of his trousers. He turned with leaden feet towards the doorway, the dread that had filled him for most of the morning dissipating as he saw Sarah, his best friend's fiancé, walking through the doorway and down the aisle towards them both, his best friend tearing up at the sight of his bride to be.

Luca knew that he did not need to worry, Sarah had given him no reason to think that she wouldn't show up on her wedding day, and yet he was unable to stop his mind from going back to another wedding, another time. Although it had been three years since Cassandra had left Luca standing at the altar, he had remained single. He had spent hours rehashing what should have been the happiest day of their lives and was no closer to finding an answer than he was three years ago.

He knew that Cassandra had been a bit out of sorts in the days leading up to their wedding, but he had put it down to wedding jitters, had listened to his relatives when they told him he had nothing to worry about, that Cassandra would talk to him if she had any worries. They had been wrong.

Luca had waited at the end of the aisle for over an hour before the reality of the situation had dawned on him. Cassandra was not showing up. Luca had slipped away into the vestry, had called Cassandra on her mobile phone, frowning as it went straight to voicemail. Message after message was left to no avail. His mobile phone had remained silent.

As if in a daze, Luca had sent everyone home, had ignored concerned glances and kind offers of company, and had returned, alone, to the apartment that he shared with Cassandra. Eventually, after a month of waiting and hoping, Luca had to face the truth. Cassandra had left him, without explanation, and had no intention of coming back.

Luca had packed up their Brisbane apartment, placed all of their belongings into storage, and travelled around the world doing short stints of consulting work and teaching. At twenty-eight, he had already reached the rank of surgical consultant, with a special interest in rural health, and his skills were in high demand. It had kept him busy, helped fill the void left behind by Cassandra, and most importantly, had kept Luca from thinking too long about her.

Luca had not heard from her since, he wondered if he ever would. Cassandra had been an only child, with no living relatives when she and Luca had met. He had been in medical school, and she had been working as a bartender to fund an overseas holiday. Their connection had been instant, within six months they had moved in together and his family had embraced her as if she had always been a part of them.

His friends had become her friends, and with no living relatives, no one had heard from her. Luca often wondered if they had rushed things, if they had really known each other at all. He shook his head to clear away his thoughts, focusing instead on his best friend as he pledged to love, honour, and obey Sarah. As best man, Luca stayed until the end of the reception, acting as a congenial and delighted wedding guest, only a very few attending knew how he really felt.

Having seen Ben and Sarah off on their honeymoon, Luca returned to his borrowed home, where he again started to pack his suitcases. He had loved his time in London, had graciously been put up by Ben and Sarah, but his three-month stint was up. If he was being honest, he was growing tired of the constant relocating and was almost looking forward to his next assignment.

**Keep reading for an extract from
"A Christmas Hope".**

A Christmas Hope
Extract

Louise looked at the empty chair across the table from her and sighed. Where was he? He had promised that he would not be late, that tonight, he would be here, and he would be on time. Louise should have known better than to get her hopes up. Knowing Jack, he had most likely forgotten, Louise not rating very high on his list of priorities anymore.

She sighed again, looking surreptitiously around the crowded room for any sign of her errant husband. It hadn't always been this way, her life had not always been an endless rotation of lunches and charity events, there was a time when Jack and Louise were carefree, when it was Louise who worked, and Jack who depended on her.

Married straight out of high school, they had lived in a horrible little dump of a flat, only made bearable by the fact that they had each other. Louise had worked as a waitress in a small restaurant while Jack had studied medicine at the local university, going on to specialise in general medicine with an emphasis on rural health.

Louise had always intended to go to university herself one day, it just never happened. Every penny she made went to cover all of the bills and expenses, but she never regretted it, not once. Louise had loved Jack, she would have done anything for him, without question.

She just didn't realise the toll being married to a doctor would take on her relationship. With Jack a partner in an inner-city practice now, things were better, financially, yet for Louise at least, things were much worse personally. Back when they were starting out and had nothing to their names, they had had each other, and they had had love. They had spruced up their horrible little dump of a flat with thrift shop finds and had enjoyed living there together. Now Louise knew that no matter how much she filled their luxury penthouse apartment with items, it would never be home or cosy, or even filled with love.

While Jack worked long hours, Louise tried to keep herself busy by volunteering at the local library, reading to children and helping out with the homework centre. She found a lot of joy in helping out with the homework centre, a place where children could come after school, instead of going home to an empty house, and get help with their homework until their parents finished work and collected them.

It gave Louise purpose, and she had always adored children. Maybe in another life, she would have worked as a teacher or held her own babies in her arms. Louise swallowed the sudden thickness in her throat. She would not cry, not here, not ever. Tears hadn't helped her before, nothing had.

Jack was in his last year of residency, rotating through the emergency department when Louise had first started bleeding. Although her pregnancy had been unplanned, both she and Jack had been thrilled with the prospect. By the time Jack had finally returned Louise's calls, she had already been admitted into the maternity ward and had lost their baby. She had gone through it alone, Jack urging her not to announce the pregnancy until she was in the second trimester. Louise had disagreed, she knew that had anything gone wrong she would want the support of her family and friends, but she had, eventually, gone along with Jack.

After she lost the baby, she hadn't spoken to anyone, her family still had no idea that she had even been pregnant. That was almost six years ago, and Jack had barely touched her since, going out of his way to avoid any physical contact. At first, Louise hadn't cared, but the longer it dragged on, the more she had grown to resent, and then hate him for it. Louise had tried confronting him over it, but he had refused to talk about it.

The last time Jack had touched Louise was almost five weeks ago. He had been out with friends after work and had arrived home drunk. He had told Louise that she was beautiful and had surprised her by kissing her. She had thought that finally, things were starting to get back to normal between them, but the following day Jack had untangled himself from her, unable to make eye contact. He had actually apologized to Louise, promising her that there would be no repercussions, that he would write her out a script for the morning-after pill, which he did, leaving it on her bedside table before going to shower for work.

It was at that moment that Louise felt her heart crack in two, the physical pain in her chest so bad she thought that she would literally die from it. Somehow, she had found the strength to get up and move, by the time Jack had finished in the shower, Louise was gone. They hadn't spoken since except via text messages.